NIGHT OF THE LIVING BREAD

SUGAR AND SPICE MYSTERIES
BOOK FOUR

MARY LEE ASHFORD

Cover art by Dar Albert at Wicked Smart Designs

Published by Oliver-Heber Books

0 9 8 7 6 5 4 3 2 1

For friends old and new, near and far.
True friends are the real riches in life

"You are such a sucker." My business partner and bestie, Dixie Spicer, pointed a finger at me. Albeit it was a finger tipped with a dollop of chocolate frosting, which made it difficult to take her seriously, but that was beside the point.

It's true. I am a sucker.

I'm a sucker for little kids with lemonade stands, old ladies selling daffodils, and any and all varieties of animal rescue fundraisers. Adopt a dog, save a cat, dollars for donkeys. They see me coming a mile away.

"Sugar, it's impossible for you to say no." Dixie had spotted the frosting and licked it from her finger.

"I can, too." Picking up a spoon, I reached in front of her and dipped some frosting from the bowl. Why fool around with only a finger of frosting? You've got to lean in.

Yum. I sighed in ecstasy.

The rich dark chocolate was pure bliss.

And it would nicely complement the praline pecan

cupcakes cooling on the counter. A test recipe for our latest project, a community cookbook for the local band boosters.

Dixie swatted my spoon away, but a smile quirked her lips.

I'd grown up in cities but was madly in love with the small town where I'd lived for the past couple of years. I cherished the friendships, the simplicity, and the slower pace. It was perfect for someone looking for fewer distractions and a sense of belonging. And ideal for the types of cookbooks that we produced at Sugar & Spice Publishing.

"The *Tasty Notes Cookbook* will make them money and still turn a profit for us." I reached in for another spoonful of frosting. "I ran the numbers, and we're good."

"Agreed." Dixie touched a couple of the cupcakes and, apparently deciding they were cool enough to frost, picked up a knife and scooted the bowl of frosting out of my reach. "You've got a much better head for business than I do, but you're still a sucker."

"Speaking of business—" I was about to fill her in on my meeting with Marla Mercer, the Jameson County Historical Society's chair, when the bell over the front door of our shop dinged.

Tina Martin, the real estate agent from a couple of doors down, popped through the door. As usual, Tina was color-coordinated to the nth degree. Today's theme was autumn, with a burnt orange jacket over a brown dress and, of course, deep crimson fingernails.

"You girls are not going to believe this." Tina leaned in and lowered her voice, though we were the only ones in the shop.

"Believe what?" I leaned in too. I'm also a sucker for secrets.

"I'm not supposed to say who, but ..." Tina paused for

effect. "A certain celebrity chef is coming through St. Ignatius in a few weeks."

My mind pinged from cooking show to cooking show. It was too much to ask that someone from my favorite, *The Great British Baking Show*, would be making a stop in our small Midwest town. More likely, it would be someone from *Baking Takes the Cake* or *Food Fight*.

"Well, don't leave us in suspense, Tina." With a flourish of her knife, Dixie swiped more frosting on the cupcake in her hand and held it out to Tina. "Who is it?"

Tina reached for the cupcake, but Dixie held it aloft, her height giving her an advantage.

"I'm not supposed to …"

"We know." Dixie waited. "So give us a hint."

"His name starts with Dino, and he loves fried food," she blurted out.

Dixie handed Tina the cupcake with a smile.

Note to self: Don't ever trust Tina with a secret.

The celebrity coming through St. Ignatius had to be the one and only extravagantly mean Dino Diner, who had his own television show about roaming the continental US looking for the best of the best diner food. And though I was definitely a fan of diner fare and especially our local Red Hen Diner, I was not a fan of Dino.

"Isn't that exciting?" Tina took a dainty nibble of the cupcake.

"Mmmm," I said, turning to grab a tray for the remaining cupcakes that Dixie was making short work of icing.

She gave me a questioning look as she slid another onto the tray. "I'd think this would be right up your alley."

"Hmmm." I went for noncommittal again. If you can't say something nice, don't say anything at all. That's what my Aunt

Cricket and Southern upbringing had taught me. I tried my best to stick to it—most of the time.

"What's going on with those barricades out on County Line Road?" I asked. Tina was relatively easy to distract, and she always knew what was happening in every part of the community.

"Problem with a water line break." She took another dainty bite.

At this rate, it was going to take a couple of hours for her to finish that cupcake. I admired her restraint, but that chocolate-topped praline pecan temptation would have been long gone if I'd had it in my hand. "Not a big one, but they had to dig to find it."

"Oh, are those properties not on their own well water?" I asked.

"Most used to be, but the Rural Water Association came through several years back and ran lines to all the farms, so they're supplied by the same water plant we are." Dixie finished the last of the cupcakes with a flourish and spun the tray around with satisfaction.

There was still a bit of that delicious dark chocolate frosting in her bowl, and I grabbed it before she could do something rash. Like wash it.

"They are, and most are happy to have the convenience. Wells can be unreliable if you have a dry year." Tina nibbled again.

For the love of Pete, was the woman never going to finish that cupcake? And how was it even possible to take such tiny bites?

"Well, except for that grumpy Dwayne Darling," Dixie noted, raising a brow as she saw me reach for the spoon. "He wasn't happy with the water line going across his field, but that's the only way they could get to the farm behind him."

"He eventually allowed it, though. Poor man." Tina was finally finishing up her treat and looked around for a napkin to wipe her fingers. Dixie handed her a paper towel.

"Why 'poor man'?" I had rummaged under the counter and found an open box of graham crackers. The perfect foundation for chocolate frosting.

"Oh, his wife, Delores, disappeared ten, maybe twelve years ago, and he never heard from her again. No one did." Tina had cleaned her hands and dropped the paper towel in the trash and now looked to be heading out the door. Probably had other stops to make to share her inside intel about the town's visit from a celebrity chef.

"Wait." I stopped with a frosting-laden graham cracker halfway to my mouth. "Delores Darling?"

Tina nodded.

"That's wild." I took a bite. Not a nibble, mind you. Dixie and Tina waited expectantly for me to be able to talk again.

"When I was at the Jameson County Historical Society earlier, her name came up. There was this recipe book ..."

"Well, I'd better get going." Tina waved on her way to the door and quickly exited. I noted she was not headed in the direction of her office. So my guess was she was moving on down the row of shops in order to share her "secret" scoop.

"I guess she wasn't interested in my story." I shrugged.

"I'm interested." Dixie sat on one of the stools, elbows on the counter, chin on her hands.

"I guess it wasn't that interesting." I sighed. "But regarding this cookbook, they're wanting to create recipes for old-fashioned breads. Apparently, they started a project like that once before and the person heading it up was none other than Delores Darling. Crazy, huh?"

"Are there really enough bread recipes for a whole cookbook?" Dixie seemed skeptical.

"I think there are, especially if we include sweet breads and things like cornbread and the like." I closed up the box of graham crackers and pushed the now-almost-empty bowl out of my reach. "And with all the notes on the project from when they started before, it should be easy-peasy."

"Easy-peasy, huh?" Dixie had put away all of her ingredients and moved her utensils to the sink. "Are you ready for lunch? Or did all that frosting spoil your appetite?"

"As you know, nothing really spoils my appetite." I wiped down the counter and dried my hands. "Red Hen?"

"You know it." She grinned. The diner was our go-to and for good reason. The food was phenomenal, the prices were great, and the owner, Toy George, made sure everything ran like clockwork. I only hoped Dino Diner would think so too.

I stopped for a moment, looking down at my black pants and favorite off-white cardigan.

"What's wrong?" Dixie asked.

"Nothing's wrong per se." I frowned. "It's just that after Tina has been here, I feel so shlumpy." I pulled at the waistband of my pants. "I probably need to give up dessert for a month, and I definitely need to get back to my morning runs."

"Yeah, right." She put her hands on her hips. "What I wouldn't give for that cute, slim figure."

"And what I wouldn't give for your height," I shot back.

Why do we always wish for what we don't have?

"You sell yourself short, Sugar." Dixie shook her head.

"I don't know. I look at someone like Tina and I feel so plain."

"Amazing, thick, dark hair, seriously perfect porcelain skin, smoke-gray eyes." She ticked them off on her fingers. "And those eyelashes? To die for. I wouldn't call that plain by a long shot."

"Vibrant curls, adorable freckles, and sparkly green eyes," I returned. "I'll stop selling myself short if you'll stop acting like you're not gorgeous."

She hesitated for a beat, taking in my point.

As women, we easily slipped into being self-critical. Focusing on what we didn't have. As Dixie had said, selling ourselves short.

I could see the shift in thinking on her face.

"Okay, deal. I'm gorgeous." She laughed, linking her arm through mine. "Let's go, beautiful."

"You got it." I grabbed my bag. "Want to take bets on whether Tina has made her way there with her secret or someone else has beat her to it?"

We stepped out of the front of the shop and onto the sidewalk. The Red Hen Diner was across the town square from Sugar & Spice Cookbooks, only a short walk away, and it was a beautiful fall day.

As we stepped off the curb at the corner to cross the street, a skateboarder nearly mowed us down.

"Hey, watch it!" I called to the kid as I jumped out of his way.

"Sorry." He turned his head and looked back with a grimace of apology just as two other skateboarders swerved around us on each side to join him.

"They're not even supposed to be on the sidewalk," Dixie commented, looking around to see whether there were more.

"No kidding. And think if it had been Greer or any of the

ladies from The Good Life. They would likely have taken a tumble."

"True." Dixie shook her head. "That was some fancy footwork on your part."

~

"Cluck," the Red Hen Diner's door chime announced as we stepped in. The diner's décor was chicken themed and kitschy but in a good way. The aroma of fresh-brewed coffee and the chatter of the packed restaurant greeted us.

Toy George already had two menus in hand and motioned us to follow her to a booth in the back corner. "Coffee?" she asked, pointing at me. "And milk or lemonade?" She looked at Dixie.

"Lemonade," Dixie answered, and in short order, Toy was back with our drinks.

Toy wiped her hands on her red-checkered apron and slid into the booth beside Dixie. "So what do you two know about this celebrity guy who's coming to town?"

"Only what Tina didn't tell us." Dixie laughed. "You know, because it's a 'secret.'" She gave an exaggerated wink.

"I understand he travels around eating at diners, and from what I've heard, I'm not sure I want him to eat at mine." Toy made a face.

"I'm sure he'll love the Red Hen as much as we do." Dixie smiled and pushed the menu back in Toy's direction. "I'll have the club sandwich with a side of ranch dressing for my fries."

"And you?" Toy turned my way.

"I'll have the meatloaf sandwich, and no fries for me today."

Toy got to her feet and, jotting down our order, headed to the back to hand it off to the kitchen.

As soon as she was out of earshot, Dixie looked at me. "So what are you not saying? What do you know about Dino Diner?"

I guessed I needed to come clean.

"I know he's an a— uhm, not my favorite person, and he was at least part of the reason I got booted out of my job."

"Ahh, that explains your reaction." Dixie sipped her lemonade. "Do you think he's going to trash the Red Hen?"

"I can't imagine anyone having a problem with Toy or the food." I glanced around at the packed diner, which was beginning to fill with the lunch crowd. "But you never know with Dino. He doesn't get those high ratings for being nice."

"Well, even if he's not impressed, it won't impact Toy's business." She looked around the restaurant, and I followed suit.

Even as a newcomer, I'd been eating at the Red Hen long enough that I could name most of the people I saw.

"These are regulars." Dixie shrugged. "Most of these folks have been coming here for years."

"You're probably right." I shifted my coffee cup to the side as our food had already arrived. "But I hate to see someone as nice as Toy be treated badly for ratings' sake."

"I bet she's up to it." Dixie waved a fry in my direction. "You don't deal with people day in and day out without developing a tough skin. And besides, maybe he'll love it."

"I sure hope you're right." I picked up my meatloaf sandwich.

I wished I felt better about the prospects.

~

BACK AT THE OFFICE, DIXIE DOVE INTO FINALIZING THE RECIPE list for the *Tasty Notes Cookbook* for the St. Ignatius High School Band Boosters.

I was expecting a call from Liz, our graphic designer, to discuss the final layout. I also needed to call Max Windsor, who was our photographer and my …

Friend? I guessed I'd call him my friend.

Everyone else seemed ready to call him more than a friend. Dixie, Greer, probably most of the folks at the Red Hen Diner. If I were honest, I guessed in my heart I would call him more than a friend, but though we'd fallen into an easy dating-dinners-sometimes-more relationship … most importantly, Max was a wonderful friend.

I finished my call with Liz and was thrilled with the design she'd come up with for the band booster book. Her creativity mixed with Dixie's ability to select different but doable recipes. And, of course, paired with Max's amazing photos. That was what made the community cookbooks we produced at Sugar & Spice a cut above the rest.

A few emails later, I looked at my watch. Time to call Max. Scrolling to his number, I put my phone on speaker so I could take notes.

"Hello, Sugar," he said when he picked up.

"Hey, Max." His deep voice always gave me a little zing. "Where are you? You sound funny. I'm getting kind of an echo."

"Maybe that's because I'm walking in your back door."

I turned to see a grinning Max standing outside my office.

And the view was nice. Striking, piercing blue eyes, dark hair shot through with silver, dark eyelashes, and slight stubble on his jaw. And even better, he was holding out a coffee.

"I thought we were going to call. Did I get that wrong?" I asked, reaching for the coffee.

"I had some things to take care of in town." He stepped in, slid into the chair by my desk, and crossed his jean-clad legs. "So I thought I'd stop by instead and see you in person. And, by the way, your person is looking lovely today."

Blushing, I lifted the lid and sniffed the steaming liquid. "Where'd you get the coffee?"

I knew "thank you" was the right response to Max's comment, but compliments were difficult for me. I was working on it, though.

"Java Junction, a new coffee shop where the bakery used to be." He took a sip from his own cup. "I got you a maple cinnamon latte. Hope you like it?"

"Hmm. I love it." The flavors, spicy and sweet, blended well together. "What did you get?"

"An"—Max held up the cup to look at the writing on the side—"apple crisp macchiato."

"I hope they do well on that corner." Moving some files, I cleared a spot for us to work. "It's been empty for a while."

"Sugar?" Dixie poked her head through my door and spotted my visitor. "Oh, hi, Max."

"Sorry I didn't bring you anything from the new coffee shop," he apologized. "All they had was coffee."

"Don't be a Mr. Smarty Pants." She grinned at Max and then turned to me. "Sugar, I'm running home to let Moto out. My neighbor can't do it today."

"You could've brought him." I smiled. Dixie's dog was a sweetheart. "He's such a good boy."

"He is," she agreed. "But I didn't know about this when I left this morning. Something came up and she had to go pick up her daughter and won't be home in time for Moto's after-noon break."

"No worries." I hoped maybe she'd bring Moto when she came back.

Max and I got to work, and by the time Dixie returned (sadly without Moto), we'd finished reviewing the notes from my call with Liz, gone over pages and plans, and walked through the remaining timeline. I felt like we were in good shape.

"I have the photos almost ready and can stop by with them in the next few days." Max rose and stretched, his arms over his head. "Should I send them to Liz as well?"

"No, she said not to." I also stood, moving around, shaking out my arms and legs. "She wants us to wait and send them once we've made our selections."

"I hate to rush, but I've got an appointment in …" He looked at his watch. "Fifteen minutes."

"You'd better get moving." I smiled. "Is it close?"

"The little white church north of town on the highway." Max packed up. "Not sure what they have in mind, but I agreed to meet with them."

I walked with him to the back door.

"Thanks again for the coffee." I gave him a hug. "Good luck at the church."

I headed back to my office, where I found Dixie perched on my desk.

"Looking at churches?" She grinned. "Is there something you need to tell me?"

"Oh, stop." I tapped her on the knee. "And get off my desk."

"You should be nicer to me." She jumped down. "I brought you ice cream from Scoops."

"What did you get me?" Scoops ice cream is made on-site and has a revolving mix of flavors.

"The flavor of the day was red velvet." She produced two to-go cups. "So that's what we're having."

"Deal." I held out my hand.

After our ice cream break, we settled in for the afternoon. Each in our own world, working on our parts of different projects, Dixie experimenting with a recipe for cranberry chocolate chip cookies for an upcoming event at the public library.

I wasn't the only sucker.

I spent my time going over my notes for my meeting with Marla Mercer at the county historical society the next morning.

Before we knew it, it was time to call it quits. I climbed into my Jeep and waved at Dixie, who was getting into her truck. Turning the Jeep toward home, I gave a satisfied sigh. I couldn't have been happier that I no longer worked in the corporate world with its frantic pace and focus on getting ahead, with no time to catch your breath. Rolling down my window and taking a deep inhale of fresh, clean air, I smiled. Maybe Dino Dinelli had done me a favor.

My Aunt Cricket would've said I was "feeling finer than frog hair." And I was.

It had been a fine day.

I loved my adopted town, but on top of that, I adored autumn in the Midwest. Fall colors and crunchy leaves, crisp air and apple cider, pumpkin patches and cozy sweaters. What wasn't to love?

When I arrived for our meeting, the grounds of the Jameson County Historical Complex were bathed in morning light, and the leaves were in the midst of changing color on the tall trees that surrounded the main building. The sun's rays picked out burnt orange, deep red, and soft yellow. Absolutely gorgeous.

Taking a deep breath of fresh fall air, I stopped for a moment and looked around. It wasn't hard to imagine what life might have looked like when folks in Jameson County shopped at a general store, children attended a one-room school, and people communicated not via text but through letters mailed at a post office like the replica that sat off to one side.

I'd agreed to this early morning meeting because Marla Mercer, the chair of the historical society, had insisted that this was the only time she was available. She was an efficient lady and wanted to get this project moving. I could appreciate a no-nonsense mentality.

Following Marla's directions around to the back, I brought my thoughts back to the present, remembering all the buzz about Dino Dinelli and his visit that I'd heard yesterday. I couldn't get over the idea that the town's tourism committee thought it was a good idea to bring the *Dino's Diners* show to St. Ignatius. Good grief. Had they never watched his show?

Though, when I thought about it, I realized I hadn't watched the show for a while. A while being the amount of time since I'd been downsized, or "dumped," as Dino termed it when he came across a diner that didn't meet his extremely subjective and often thought-up-in-the-moment standards. In any case, it was my time as a magazine food editor and a particular run-in with Dino that accounted for my low opinion of the *Diners* host.

Okay, let it go. No need to anticipate trouble. Focus on the present and the positive.

Shaking my head to clear it, I made my way to the back entrance. There were a couple of cars in the staff parking lot, so I assumed Marla had already arrived. I knew she was anxious to see the proposal before I presented it to the rest of the historical society board. So I hoped I'd hit the right mark with what I'd pulled together after a very late night.

As I climbed the three steps that led to the door, I could see that it was wide open. I tapped on the windowpane before entering and called, "Hello?"

Racine, the young woman who was the docent, stood in the middle of the kitchen area.

"Hello. You're here early." I smiled at her.

Racine opened her mouth but didn't speak.

"I was supposed to meet Marla," I explained.

She tried again, but no words came out.

I stepped forward. "Are you okay?"

She managed to shake her head. "No," she croaked.

With a shaky hand, she pointed at the floor, and as I rounded the corner of the counter, I could see Marla on the floor.

"Oh, no." I knelt down. "Did she pass out? Have you called 9-1-1?"

"N-no," Racine stumbled backward.

I reached into my bag and dialed the emergency number, then shifted so I could check out what had happened to Marla and whether she was okay.

That's when I noticed the very large bread knife sticking out of Marla's back.

"9-1-1, what's your emergency?" A voice came on my phone.

"I'm at the Jameson County Historical Complex at ..." I looked to Racine for the address.

She shrugged.

"I don't have the address," I explained to the woman on the line. "We're in the main building at the back entrance, which is open. We have an injured woman, Marla Mercer, who has been ..." I swallowed hard and took a deep breath. "Has been stabbed."

"I'll send an ambulance."

"It may be too late for that. You may want to send the sheriff."

As it turned out, the ambulance and the sheriff arrived quickly and at about the same time. The Jameson County Historical Complex is at the south edge of town and not really near any residential areas. So I'm not sure how we'd collected such a big crowd in that short of a time. I could hear the chatter outside the door and wasn't looking forward to the questions. I was sure they were mostly questions I couldn't answer. In fact, I had plenty of questions of my own.

I stood to one side as the emergency medical folks did their due diligence, though I could tell from the nods, grave expressions, and lack of urgency that there wasn't really any hope for Marla.

Sheriff Terrance Griffin leaned against the counter, waiting for the EMTs to finish. I usually referred to him as Sheriff Terry. He'd told me to call him Terry, but it didn't seem right when he was in uniform.

He looked up and spotted me. I could almost hear the sigh from across the room as he wiped a hand across his face and headed my way.

"Cookbook project?" he asked.

I nodded. "County historical society. Vintage bread recipes."

He looked at me, looked back at the EMTs, and when one of them shook her head, sighed again. "Killed with a bread knife."

"So she's …" I had been pretty sure, but hearing it confirmed made me swallow hard. "She's …"

"Yes. Dead." He took my arm and steered me away from Marla, giving the emergency crew room to pack up. "Are you the one who found her?"

"Yes. Well, no." I stumbled over my words. "Racine was here when I got here."

The sheriff raised a brow and looked around. "Racine?"

"She's the docent, and she was here when I arrived."

"Was she inside or outside?"

"Inside," I responded.

Sheriff Griffin didn't have a pen and paper, but I could tell he was taking notes in his head.

"Do you know where she is now?"

I shrugged. When I thought about it, I realized that I hadn't seen Racine since my 9-1-1 call. I'd assumed that she'd gone outside to direct the paramedics when they arrived. Maybe she was still outside and dealing with crowd control. I could tell the numbers were growing by the increase in volume of the chatter.

"Do you want me to find her?" I needed something to do.

"No." He held up his hand. "You stay put. I'm going to have Deputy Butters take your statement while everything is fresh in your mind. I'll find Racine."

I thought it might be easier if I looked for her since I knew what she looked like. But I didn't share that thought, as I knew from previous experience that our friendly county sheriff didn't take kindly to advice from civilians. Even if it was helpful and well intended.

The paramedics were all packed up, and the crime scene techs had arrived. Looking around for a place to sit, I shifted my bag to my other arm and, in the process, smacked a red-haired deputy in the tush.

"Oh, ah, sorry," I mumbled.

"Apology accepted," he replied, his cheeks turning pink. "Deputy Butters." He held out his hand.

I shifted the bag again so I could shake his hand. "Ah, you're going to take my statement."

He nodded and indicated a corner where we would be out of the way of the activity in the kitchen. He pulled out a pad of paper and a pen.

"So you arrived and found the victim on the floor?" he prompted.

"I arrived, and the door was open," I began. "And I knocked."

He raised a brow.

"On the windowpane," I continued. "And Racine was standing in the middle of the kitchen area. And—"

"What's Racine's last name?"

This was going to take a long time if Deputy Butters kept interrupting.

"It's …" Oh, no. I couldn't remember her last name. Did I even know it? I tried to recall whether Marla had used it when introducing us.

"It's 'Middlebrooks,'" a male voice behind me offered.

"That's it! Middlebrooks." I turned to see Lewis Brimley, the vice-chair of the historical society, who gave me a flirty wink.

I did a double take. Did that just happen?

Ohmigosh, I think I was just hit on by a guy at least twice my age and, even worse, at a murder scene.

"Where did you come from?" I asked.

"I was out there." The older man ran a hand through his silver hair and pointed toward the door. "Quite a crowd. I stepped in to see if I could help with anything." He looked toward Deputy Butters.

"Hello, Officer." He held out his hand. "I'm Lewis, the vice-chair of the St. Ignatius Historical Society." He said it with all the importance of a visiting diplomat. "Do you need anything from me?"

"There are some areas that we need to get into that are locked." Deputy Butters stopped writing on his paper. "Do you have keys?"

"I know where they're kept." Lewis nodded. "I can show you."

The deputy waved Sheriff Griffin over, and after a brief consultation, the sheriff and Lewis headed back into a hallway that led to the rest of the building. I turned back to Deputy Butters, and we began again.

We'd no sooner gotten through the "I came in and saw Racine and then found Marla" part than there was shouting from outside.

A tall woman—and I do mean tall—was being held back by one of the other deputies, who was losing the battle to keep her from coming through the doorway.

Deputy Butters sprinted across the room and blocked the door.

She shoved him aside. He stumbled and fell toward where the crime scene techs were working. The other deputy tackled the woman, but just as it looked like he was going to be put in a headlock, Sheriff Griffin burst into the room.

"What the hell is going on here?" he barked.

Everyone, including the crime scene techs, the tall woman, and the two deputies, started talking at once.

I knew when not to chime in.

"Ollie and Dean," he said, pointing toward the two deputies, "outside."

They scrambled to their feet and wasted no time exiting.

"Mame, I can't let you in here until the crew is done." Sheriff Terry turned her away from Marla's body, and his voice softened. "I'm so sorry. Let's go through here."

He pointed to the hallway he'd come from, and amazingly, she followed his direction without a fuss.

The sheriff's gaze suddenly landed on me.

"Sugar, did Deputy Butters finish taking your statement?"

"Sort of." I wasn't sure the deputy would agree, but I'd really told him everything I could.

"You can go ahead and take off, but I wouldn't go out that way if I were you." He tipped his head toward the door.

I wasn't wild about leaving that way myself. I peered outside, where the crowd seemed to have settled down. However, they had pushed right up against the yellow tape that had been put up to keep them from getting too close.

"Come on." He motioned for me to follow the tall woman. "I'll show you another way out."

$\mathcal{I}$ sat in my office at Sugar & Spice Publishing and flipped through my notes and papers for the historical society project without really seeing them. One part of my brain was in total shock that Marla Mercer was dead.

The other part of my brain kept going over the scene. What did I see? What could I remember? What could have happened to Marla? Did it look like there had been an argument? A struggle?

I'd met Marla only recently, but she was, without a doubt, one of the sweetest women I'd ever encountered. It seemed like everyone liked her. I couldn't imagine anyone having a problem with Marla and certainly not a big enough problem to stab her.

Then it had to be an intruder, which was scary. Or a random act, which was even scarier.

"Sugar? Hello …" I looked up to see Dixie standing in the doorway. "You must be deep in thought. You didn't even hear me come in."

"I didn't." I shuffled through the papers and then mindlessly tucked them back in the folder.

"What's all the hubbub at the historical complex?" Dixie moved to hang up her jacket. "It looked like a crowd out there. Was there a fire or something? That would be a shame with all those archives. Bertie used to be on the board. She kept telling them they need to digitize."

"Worse."

Dixie waited for me to compose myself.

"Marla Mercer is dead."

"Dead?"

"She was stabbed."

"Stabbed? Ohmigosh! But you were going there to drop off the cookbook proposal."

I nodded.

Her face changed, and I could see the realization hit her. "You found her, didn't you?"

Dixie immediately went into care mode. And she knew me, so she headed for the coffee maker in our test kitchen.

Soon she was back with a big cup of coffee and a cranberry chocolate chip cookie for me. And a glass of milk and another cookie for herself. Setting the food and drink down on the edge of the desk, she settled into one of the chairs.

"Okay, talk me through it." She leaned forward.

I talked her through my arrival, the door being open, and me walking in and seeing Racine, then Marla. The phone call to 9-1-1 and the arrival of the sheriff and deputies. And lastly, the tall, upset woman bursting in.

"I thought Sheriff Terry called her 'Mame,' but he could have just said 'ma'am.' There was a lot going on."

"'Mame' would be right. That'd be Mame Reinhart." Dixie

took a drink of her milk. "She and Marla were best friends. They had been for years."

"No wonder she was so distraught, then."

"And come to think of it, they were both Weavers." She set her glass on the edge of the desk.

"Like they wove things?" I asked, illustrating with my hands.

Dixie rolled her eyes. "No, like I think they were distant cousins of some sort."

"But Marla's name was 'Mercer.' Had she been married, then?"

"'Mercer' is from her dad's family. Her mother was a Weaver. And the same with Mame." She scratched her head. "I think I've got that right."

There was a tap at the back door, and Dixie got to her feet just as her brother, Hirsh, poked his head in.

"Hi, Sis. Hi, Sugar." He stepped inside.

He was dressed up. Well, dressed up for Hirsh, anyway. Usually, when I saw him, he was in jeans and work boots. Dixie's brother had his own construction company but also helped out at the Spicer family farm. Today, he was wearing khaki pants and clean running shoes and sporting a red T-shirt that said, "YAP."

"What's up?" Dixie sat back down and motioned him to come into the office.

He reached back for the door and opened it wider to reveal three boys, who also stepped inside. I wasn't great at guessing ages, but maybe "young men" would have been the better term. Perhaps "high school freshman"? The precise term was hard to pinpoint for boys that age. They were all wearing T-shirts that matched Hirsh's.

I thought the tallest of the kids looked familiar, but I

wasn't sure where I'd seen him. He was tall and lanky, with a distinctive forward mop of curly, dark hair.

"We're here to ask for a favor." Hirsh stepped to one side and swept his arm toward the three. "Go ahead, guys."

There was a lot of throat clearing and looking at the floor, but then, finally, the one closest to Hirsh spoke up. "We're looking for—"

"Wait." Hirsh held up his hand. "Why don't you introduce yourselves first."

"I'm Zac," said the tall one. He hitched a thumb toward the sandy-haired guy next to him. "He's Gil. And that's Bruce." He leaned forward a bit and pointed to the short, towheaded kid on the end.

He looked at Hirsh, who nodded. "We're doing a fundraiser—" Zac began.

"And you're with what organization, and why are you doing a fundraiser?" Hirsh prompted, pointing at his "YAP" T-shirt.

The boy sighed. "We're part of the St. Ignatius Youth Advisory Program." He looked at Hirsh for approval. "And we're doing this fundraiser thing to get enough money to build a skate park here in town. And the land's already been donated, but we have to get enough money to do the design and build it and stuff."

It all came out in a rush, like he was afraid Hirsh would interrupt him again. Which was a distinct possibility. But as he was speaking, I realized where I'd seen the tall kid, Zac. He was the one who had almost mowed me down on his skateboard yesterday when we were on our way to the Red Hen Diner.

I met his baby-blue gaze, and he looked away. Ah, he remembered too.

"What kind of a fundraiser are you doing?" Dixie asked. Either she didn't recognize the kid or was pretending she didn't.

"I'm guessing you're not putting together a cookbook." I smiled at them.

"No," Zac finally spoke up. "We're doing an auction at the Fall Festival."

"Some of the businesses have donated items," Hirsh broke in to explain. "But since you two don't actually sell a product directly, we were hoping you could donate cookies."

"Absolutely," I agreed, full well knowing that it was going to be Dixie doing the baking. "What's your favorite cookie?"

"Chocolate chip!" the trio responded as one.

"Count us in." Dixie grinned.

You could feel the collective sigh of relief as Hirsh herded the three back out the door, almost colliding with Disco, who ran Flashback, the storefront next to ours.

Today, Disco was in full '70s flair with a *Feeling Groovy* T-shirt and red-white-and-blue bell bottoms. Where did the guy find this stuff?

"Hey, dudes." Disco high-fived the trio. "Are you doing some cooking? Or maybe some tasting?" He said the last part with such hope that it was clear he was looking to do a bit of tasting himself. He was a frequent visitor and often made sure he stopped by when Dixie was baking.

Dixie had gathered up some more cookies and handed them out to the boys and Hirsh. Disco held his hands out, and she dropped a couple of cookies in them.

"Thanks, Dix, and by the way, your front door is locked," Disco said over his shoulder as he headed back out.

Dixie and I looked at each other and smiled. It was locked because we weren't open yet, but I had to wonder who was watching Disco's shop or whether perhaps his front door was locked too.

We made our way to the front of the shop and unlocked our door, though we didn't really have many customers who wandered in off the street. Most of our visitors were other merchants on the square. Occasionally, we met with potential clients at the shop.

I had started a display of previous projects in one corner so that those interested in working with us could see the various types of cookbooks that we'd created for other groups. My display was a work in progress.

Some of the best features in the room were the ginormous photos of different dishes that Max had done for us. If you weren't hungry when you arrived, you for sure would be after being surrounded by these photos—which reminded me that I was supposed to set up a time with Max to select the photos for the band booster cookbook. I was excited to see them.

WHAT A DAY. I PULLED INTO MY DRIVEWAY AND SAT IN MY CAR for a few minutes before gathering my things and heading inside. I'd started the day focused on meeting Marla and checking that off my list, but what a turn. Still unbelievable. As I made my way to the front porch and fumbled for my key, I could see the curtain in the window next door move.

Sigh. I did not need this.

I knew from experience that the curtain movement meant my neighbor, Mrs. Pickett, was watching for me to get home. And now that she'd spotted me, she would shortly be on her way over with some new complaint. Most likely about some infraction on my part. One I'd unwittingly committed, such as having leaves on my sidewalk, weeds in my yard, or noncompliant garbage containers. The woman was an HOA on steroids. Though I didn't think any homeowners' association I'd ever dealt with was anywhere near being in her league.

I thought about waiting for her on the porch, but when I heard the loud and mournful meow through the front door, I knew I'd better get inside and greet (and feed) Ernest, or there would be no end to the drama.

Sure enough, my feline roommate was standing in the hallway just inside the door and greeted me with a very dramatic and loud meow. A handsome six-toed tabby, Ernest was also proficient in glares and eye rolls and an Olympic napper.

"Ernest," I said as I put down my bag, "you are not starving. I mean, look at that belly."

At that comment, he blinked his green eyes, turned with a swish of his fluffy tail, and padded toward the kitchen. I followed obediently and pulled a container from the cupboard, filled his dish, and took his water bowl to the sink.

I had no sooner rinsed and refilled it when—*Boom! Boom! Boom!*—the pounding on my door began.

Sighing again, I headed to the front hallway.

There was no avoiding Mrs. Pickett. I figured I might as well get this over with.

Opening the door, I greeted her, "Hello, Mrs.—"

She didn't wait for me to finish but pushed past me into the foyer.

Taken aback (I didn't think she'd ever actually been inside my house), I stepped aside. She was wearing her usual pink bathrobe, which matched the pink foam curlers in her hair. As a nod to the cooler autumn weather, she had wrapped a flannel scarf around her head, and it draped enough to cover her neck as well.

"This may take a while," she declared. "We might as well go into the kitchen. Do you have tea?"

"Uhm. Sure." I thought I probably did, but I really couldn't remember what type. I was more of a coffee drinker. Following her into the kitchen, I hurriedly searched my cupboards and found some Earl Grey.

Plopping a bag in a very nice teacup (thanks, Mother), I heated some water and poured it into Mrs. Pickett's cup.

"Sugar?" She looked at me pointedly.

"Yes?" I responded.

With a major eye roll, she pointed at the counter. "No, I'd like some sugar for my tea."

"Oh." I reached for the sugar bowl and a spoon and carried them to the table. "Here you go. Do you need anything else?"

"Cut the pleasantries." She scooped two teaspoons of sugar into her tea and then looked up at me. "I need your help."

What?

I could not have been more shocked if she had told me she was a British spy.

This woman had made it clear that she had no use for me since I'd moved in. I hadn't even had time to get on her bad side (and this was assuming she had a good side) when she'd simply dismissed me as an inept renter, a careless caretaker, and pretty much an overall waste of time. And now she needed my help? For what?

"You're good at snooping." She sipped the tea very cautiously, as if I might have somehow slipped some poison in it, then set her cup down with a click. "Solving Alma Stoller's murder a while back and all." Mrs. Pickett took a deep breath and closed her eyes.

I waited, leaning with my elbows on the table.

Her eyes popped open, and she trained them on me. "Now Marla Mercer's been killed, and they think my niece, Mame, killed her."

What the ...? I nearly fell off my chair.

"I'm sure that—" I began, but she cut me off with a sharp slice of her hand.

"Nobody's sure of anything, and that young Griffin and his minions couldn't find a squirrel in a nut factory, let alone a killer."

Insulted on Sheriff Terry's behalf, I stood. "But—" I started again.

"I told Mame you'd talk to her. She'll be over about seven o'clock." She drank the last drop from her teacup and slid it back on the table.

"But—"

"No ifs, ands, or buts about it," she interrupted, getting to her feet. "My Mame is always on time. She'll be here."

"But—" I tried again.

"Seven o'clock." She pointed a bony finger at me. "I'll let myself out."

And just like that, she was gone.

Ernest and I looked at each other.

"Well, what if I wasn't going to be here?" I asked him. "What if I had plans?"

Ernest tipped his head and meowed. In agreement with me, I'm sure.

I didn't have plans, but the nerve of the woman to assume that she could make an appointment for me. And tell her niece to come to my house?

"I'll call her up and tell her it doesn't work for me," I said to Ernest, reaching for my phone.

He rolled his eyes, which I interpreted to mean, "Why would you do that?"

"You're right." I tossed the phone on the counter.

In truth, I didn't have any plans and seven worked just fine. Plus, I really did want to talk to the woman who had barged in at the historical society and been so upset by Marla's death. I had a lot of questions. Like what was her relationship with Marla? How did she learn about her death? And why did Sheriff Terry suspect her?

And one more: How on earth could the poor woman possibly be related to wacky Mrs. Pickett?

I SPENT THE NEXT HOUR TRYING TO PUT MY HOUSE IN ORDER. Or at least the visible part of it. It wasn't that I was unusually messy, but I'd had a mother who had insisted on an impeccable home. Nothing out of place, no dust, no mess, no fingerprints, which meant I had sheltered in place in my room a lot as a kid.

I thought I had overcome the perfectionism. But here I was, stress cleaning.

By the time the doorbell rang at exactly seven o'clock, I'd worked up a sweat. I'd also worked up a lot more questions. I wiped my forehead with the kitchen towel I was holding and jotted down another question on my list. I wasn't going to grill her, but I didn't want to forget any details.

"Hello." Opening the door, I held out my hand. "I'm Sugar."

"Uhm, hi." She was as tall as I remembered and towered over me. Her palm was clammy when she shook my hand, and she hesitated in the doorway as if she weren't sure about entering.

I couldn't help but compare her demeanor to earlier at the crime scene when she'd been bold and almost demanding. But I guessed if you just found out your best friend was killed, you wouldn't be at your calmest. I shuddered to think about what I'd do if something happened to Dixie.

"Come in." I motioned. "Can I get you something to drink?"

"Water would be great." She stepped in and looked around, her eyes darting back and forth. "Where should I sit?"

"Let's go in the living room." I'd thought it would be the most comfortable and hoped it would make it easier for her to relax. My Aunt Cricket would have pronounced Mame "as nervous as a cat in a room full of rocking chairs."

And speaking of cats, where had my feline disappeared to? He'd been upset by my cleaning frenzy, so I was probably in trouble with him. I'd most likely be hearing about it later.

"I'll be right back." In the kitchen, I grabbed a couple of glasses and filled them with water, then hurried back to the living room. Mame had chosen the big armchair that I usually sat in when I read. I placed her water on the side table within reach.

"Is this okay?" she asked, squeezing the black leather purse she was holding tightly on her lap.

"It's fine." I leaned forward and laid a hand on her arm. "How are you doing?"

She jerked her arm away and clutched her purse tighter.

That's when it hit me that she was by all accounts the number one murder suspect and actually could have killed Marla.

I had only the word of Mrs. Pickett (who wasn't my biggest fan, after all) that Mame was innocent. And I would take Sheriff Terry's word over my grumpy neighbor's any day.

Way to go, Sugar. Invite a killer to your house and offer refreshments. That Southern hospitality runs deep in you, doesn't it?

I settled on the far end of the couch, making sure there were no sharp objects nearby and that my phone was within reach. "So your aunt tells me that the sheriff talked to you."

"Not him." She swallowed a sip of water. "That skinny deputy."

"Deputy Butters?" I was feeling a little bit better. If it hadn't been Sheriff Terry, maybe the case wasn't as strong as Mrs. Pickett had led me to believe. "Why did he think you were involved?"

"I wasn't. I'm not," she sputtered. "I was just shooing people off her lawn and the one reporter guy called the police on me."

Shooing people off the lawn, huh?

Maybe she had more in common with her aunt than I'd first thought.

"What can you tell me about Marla?" I sipped from my own water, wishing it were something stronger. "I only recently met her."

"She was so nice. Everyone loved her." She started to tear up. "Everyone."

Well, perhaps not everyone. Someone did off the woman.

I reframed my thoughts. "Do you know of any reason someone would have wanted to hurt Marla? Had she argued with someone? Anyone new she'd been talking to or talking about?" I glanced at my list of questions.

"No. She was such a sweet person. I don't remember her ever fighting with anybody. Ever. Even when Lewis from the historical society was flirty with her and she didn't like it, she was nice to him. Even when people were rude to her, she was kind."

I bet by Lewis, she meant the silver-haired Casanova at the crime scene who had winked at me.

"Was someone recently rude to her?" Marla sounded like a saint. "Did she share anything like that?" I was careful not to fire too many questions at her, as she seemed to be relaxing a little.

"Oh, just the usual. Some of those board members at the historical society can be pretty nasty."

"About what?" I mentally flipped through what Marla had told me about the other board members.

"A couple of them thought they should have been elected chair instead of her." She humphed. "I guess they shoulda been nicer if they wanted people to vote for them."

"Like who?" I quietly picked up the pen on the table to jot a note.

"Like Karla Swindler." Mame shook her head. "Now, there's a piece of work. And she wouldn't have even been any good at it. She would've thought that Marla and the rest should have done all the work."

I wrote down the name. "And you said, 'a couple.' Was there someone else?"

"Also—"

My doorbell rang before she could finish, startling Mame. She grabbed at her purse, knocking the glass of water off the table.

Torn between helping her and answering the door, I zipped into the kitchen for paper towels, rushed back, and handed them to her.

Thankfully, it was only water and not a lot of it. We mopped up what we could.

The doorbell rang again, and I headed to answer the door.

But when I stepped into the entryway, what I saw made me want to turn off the lights and hide.

It was Sheriff Terry Griffin, and through no fault of my own, I was about to be in big trouble.

"Hello." The sheriff stepped in, and I waved him toward the living room. I thought I might as well get this over with.

He didn't seem all that surprised when he spotted Mame, who was back in her chair and back to clutching her bag.

"Water? Coffee?" I offered.

He shook his head. "I didn't realize you two knew each other." He looked back and forth from Mame to me.

"We don't." Mame and I said in unison.

"We just met today at … you know …" I didn't want to say "the crime scene" and get Mame all upset again. "The historical society," I finished.

"So a social call? A get-to-know-you visit?" Sheriff Terry raised his eyebrows and waited.

And waited.

Mame couldn't take the silence.

She stumbled over her words, and they came out in a rush. "That red-headed deputy guy said you thought I killed Marla, and I didn't. I wouldn't ever. He said I needed to go with him. And that got me all riled up. And then my aunt said I should come and talk to Sugar here because she's good at snoopin'."

Sheriff Terry shot me a look.

I shrugged.

"Well, Sugar does have a considerable talent in that area, but I'd rather you talk to me about anything to do with the case." Sheriff Terry took a step forward. "We don't have to do it at the station."

"Okay," Mame said decisively. "I'll do that." She stood, nearly lost her bag again, and grabbed for it.

This time, the fumble dumped the contents of her purse and scattered it across the floor. I reached for a lip balm, a candy bar, and a hairbrush. Mame scrambled to grab the other things and was working her way across the living room, scooping them back into her bag, when suddenly, she stilled.

A leather case had come to rest against Sheriff Griffin's toe. He picked it up and snapped it open to reveal the biggest knife I thought I'd ever seen.

"Mame." The sheriff held up the knife. "I think we'd better go have a talk at the station, after all."

The St. Ignatius Historical Society meeting was being called to order, but "order" was definitely a misnomer, as it was a lot more like semicontrolled chaos.

"The meeting will please come to order," Lewis Brimley boomed, pounding a gavel on the table for what seemed like the hundredth time.

The chaos and conversations continued to clatter around me. Catching only part of what was being said, I guessed it was mostly discussion about the death of their former chair. I'd been glad the meeting was being held in a different part of the complex than where I'd found Marla.

I'd met her at the historic farmhouse because that was where the records and archives of historical recipes were stored. Today, we were in a newer building with a well-equipped meeting room.

I was in attendance only to get a decision on whether the group wanted to continue with their cookbook project. Truthfully, I was okay either way, as we'd recently had two more projects come through the door. And based on what I was seeing, this one had the potential to be much more complicated than either of the other two.

A woman with a stern look and a tight bun sat next to Lewis, her chin propped in her hands. The name tag on her denim jacket read *Karla Swindler*. She watched the commotion around her and shook her head. Finally, raising her chin and lifting two fingers to her lips, she let out a shrill whistle that got everyone's attention. "Please, people, can we get down to business?"

The room quieted, and Lewis repeated his pronouncement. "This meeting of the St. Ignatius Historical Society is now called to order. Lewis Brimley, Vice-Chair, presiding."

I caught a couple of looks around the table. Some formality is often required to keep any kind of meeting moving. But it did seem like Lewis took his leadership role with a bloated sense of importance.

"The first order of business is to appoint a new chair." He adjusted his glasses and straightened his power-red tie.

"I nominate Karla," a woman several seats down from Lewis spoke up. And was rewarded with a glare from the vice-chair.

"I think it's too soon to talk about a replacement for Marla," said another woman from the other side of the table. I couldn't see her name from where I sat. There were several nods of agreement with her comment, and the chatter resumed.

"Wait." Jimmie LeBlanc, a local history buff, who I remembered from the St. Ignatius Founders' Day cookbook project, stood.

The room quieted again.

"Our bylaws say ..." Jimmie paused, pulled some papers from his jacket pocket, and read. "When there's a midterm vacancy, the vice-chair will complete the chair's term until the next election."

"Exactly." Lewis nodded. "All those in favor?"

There were many "ayes," though some, I had to say, seemed to have a reluctant tone to them.

"I don't think it needs a vote," Jimmie muttered, but the group had moved on, so he sat down.

Great. Coup averted. Yay.

Now I wondered where my item was on their agenda.

Thankfully, the agenda was short and I was near the top, so it didn't take long to get to me and the *Bread Basket Cookbook*.

After a heated discussion about moving forward, they agreed to continue with the cookbook project. Again, I thought some of the "aye" votes lacked enthusiasm. In any case, I thanked them, told them I'd get a contract to them by the end of the week, and left them to continue with the rest of their meeting.

I had promised Greer Gooder, my lovely landlady, that I would stop by to see her after the board meeting. Though I needed to get back to the office and get to work closing out the band booster project and get started on the historical society contract, I didn't want to miss out on Greer's take on current events. Maybe I could pick up a few insights on the historical society board.

Pulling into the parking lot at The Good Life, the retirement complex where Greer lived, I reviewed the board players in my head.

Lewis Brimley: Seemed to think he was in charge, and as it turns out, now he officially is.

Karla Swindler: A bit abrasive but did manage to keep things on track despite Lewis's tendency to pontificate.

Jimmie LeBlanc: Mr. Rules—and thank goodness for that, as I was afraid it was going to get ugly before he stepped in.

Tally Pattison: She sat next to me. I have to ask Greer whether she knows Tally. She was quiet but seemed sort of unhappy with everything that went on.

Monica Weaver: I also need to check with Greer or Dixie to see whether Monica, who is considerably younger than the other board members, is related to Mrs. Pickett's niece, Mame. Wasn't there something Dixie said about some Weavers being involved?

I wasn't surprised to see the abundance of fall decorations outside Greer's place. Greer was enthusiastic about any holiday. Her front patio looked like a truck full of seasonal merch had jackknifed and tipped over. There was a bale of hay, multiple orange jack-o'-lanterns, some gorgeous, bright mums, and a dried cornstalk a full foot taller than me. I rang the doorbell, being careful not to dislodge the giant wreath made from autumn leaves and tiny pumpkins.

"Come on in," she called. "I'm in the kitchen."

Of course she is.

Greer was in her eighties but had an energy that we all should have aspired to emulate regardless of age. And I sure hoped that when I was an octogenarian, I would be as spry as she was.

As I stepped inside, I was met with a friendly bark from her toy poodle, Frenchie, and the luscious aroma of baking bread. The yeasty smell reminded me of my childhood days in my aunt's kitchen. Though, when I thought about it, Aunt Cricket's specialty was homemade bread. The smell was the same and took me back to my childhood. Suddenly, my heart swelled and my stomach growled. Wondering whether I had a copy of Aunt Cricket's recipe, I made a mental note to check when I got home. If I did, maybe I could get Dixie to try it out.

If I didn't, I wasn't going to call my aunt and ask for it. It would lead to all kinds of questions I didn't want to answer and advice I wasn't going to take.

"Hey, there." With a couple of steps, I was in the kitchen, Frenchie on my heels.

I reached down to pet her, complimenting her on her new autumn leaf bandana and matching bow. "Look at you, girl." I scratched the soft fur on her back. "You're all decked out for fall."

Greer's place was small compared to the lovely and spacious 1890s Queen Anne I rented from her. She never complained about the lack of space. But that was Greer Gooder, the most determined optimist I'd ever run across. "Less time needed for cleaning, more time for reading," she would often say.

And she'd apparently been reading; I noted the mystery novel, with a bright-red ribbon marking where she'd left off, on the sideboard.

"It smells delicious in here." I inhaled deeply.

"Well, your new cookbook project got me thinking. I always used to bake my own bread but haven't done it in a while. I dug around and found this recipe book—more a pamphlet, really—that has some fun recipes. Our book club meets tonight, and I thought I'd take some for a treat."

"Is this what you're reading for the book club?" I picked up the book I'd spotted and turned to look at the cover. "Is it any good?"

"It's okay." She finished pulling a tray from the oven. "I need to finish it before the meeting, but I already know who the killer is."

"Don't you usually?" I stepped closer to the stove as she

pulled some butter from her refrigerator and began brushing it over the golden crust of the bread.

"Lots of times but not always." She put down the pastry brush and wiped her hands on a towel. "But enough about fictional murders. Let's talk about Marla Mercer. What happened?"

"I don't really know." I followed her to the compact living room, and we took our usual spots. Me on the couch and Greer in her easy chair, Frenchie snuggled on Greer's lap.

"But you found her, right?" Of course Greer knew I'd found the body.

"Well, kind of. Racine found her, but then I arrived and called the sheriff."

"And Marla had been stabbed?"

"Seemed to be the case. And now they are questioning Mame Reinhart, who is some relation of my/your neighbor Mrs. Pickett. She asked me to help her."

"Wilma Jean Pickett? She asked you for help? No way!"

"According to her, I'm good at snoopin'."

Greer laughed. "I would have put it differently, but yes. Yes, you are. Do they think this was a break-in or someone who had something against Marla?"

"You know Sheriff Terry." I sighed. "He really isn't saying, but from what everyone has told me, Marla was well liked. I didn't really cross paths with her. Did you know her?"

Greer leaned back in her chair and got comfy. "She lived here all her life, and I can't imagine anyone having a problem with her or her being involved in anything that might put her at risk. Nice woman."

"Was she single?" I asked.

"I think she was engaged at one point, but the guy wanted to see the world and she didn't feel like she could leave her elderly daddy, who was alone and in ill health. Her parents left her that big house and, to my understanding, quite a bit of money. Who knows what will happen with all that now? No siblings, and I'm not sure about extended family."

"I guess she left everything to Mame Reinhart." I hadn't realized the extent of what was involved in the inheritance.

"Wow." Greer shook her head. "I guess that does make for a very strong motive."

"What can you tell me about the other members of the historical society board?" I listed off the names.

"Lewis came to town maybe ten or twelve years ago. I don't remember where from, but maybe someone at the book club will know. Seems nice enough, but ..." Her voice trailed off.

"But what?" I shifted in my spot on the couch.

"Well, he's a little above it all, if you know what I mean. Thinks he's all that. He's nice-looking. Not like your handsome Max but okay." She paused. "I just don't think he ever tried to fit in. Doesn't spend his money locally. The historical society is the only thing he's involved in as far as I know."

I resisted the urge to correct the "your" part of her reference to Max, letting it slide in an effort to zero in on Lewis Brimley. "Is Lewis married? What does he do for a living?"

"Widowed when he got here. He does something at an office near the square. Insurance maybe? Or he goes there, anyway. I'm not sure he works much. Maybe he's one of those trust fund babies."

"No problems with Marla that you know of?" I could see the outsider effect in play with Lewis. I got a bit of it myself, as I'd moved to St. Ignatius only a few years ago. People in town were genuinely nice—most of them anyway—and welcoming, but unless you were born in St. Ignatius or nearby (sometimes even a couple of counties over was too far), you got the "you wouldn't understand; you're not from here" effect.

"I haven't heard of him having problems with anybody. However, Karla Swindler is a different story. That woman has problems with pretty much everyone she meets."

"What kind of problems?" I wondered whether Mame had been right about Karla wanting to be in charge but wanting others to do the work. Maybe they'd argued. Still, that seemed like a very weak motive.

"She works at her daddy's accounting firm there on the square." Greer reached for a notepad by her chair. "You probably pass it every day."

I probably did, but I didn't remember interacting with anyone from the business. "What's it called?"

"R & S Accounting." Greer smiled. "They stuck with the initials when Karla joined. 'R & S' has a better ring than 'Rush and Swindler' when you're dealing with people's money."

"I can see why that could be not quite the image you want to portray," I agreed. "But what kinds of problems does she have?"

"Mostly because she always thinks the right way is her way. And she is so rude when anyone disagrees. I don't think she's allowed back into the Red Hen since she told Toy that 'you should never serve biscuits with butter.' You can imagine how that went over."

We both chuckled. "Tally Pattison was another of the board members I met. She didn't speak up much but seemed disgruntled with everything in general."

"You nailed her. Tally doesn't have a whole lot to complain about in life, but that's never stopped her. I'm not sure why they let her on the board or why she volunteered, but mark my words, she'll have a negative take on whatever you try to do with the group's cookbook project."

"And Monica Weaver?" I thought she'd made some good points, and she seemed to be on board with the project, but I was mostly interested in her last name. "Is there a link between her and Marla?"

"There is. Marla Mercer's mother was a Weaver, and so was Mame's mother. Both lost their moms when they were young, and I think that formed a bond between them. Mame can be challenging, but Marla seemed to have unlimited patience with her."

We chatted a little more, but Greer needed to get her book read before it was time for the book club meeting, whether she knew who the killer was or not. And I needed to get back to the office and get busy. She'd promised to share the most popular theories and tidbits related to the murder that were sure to abound at her book club.

I gave her a hug and Frenchie a belly rub and headed out with several slices of tasty, warm bread but with no clearer picture as to why anyone would have wanted the very popular Marla Mercer dead.

BACK AT THE OFFICE, I FILLED DIXIE IN ON THE BOARD MEETING and the fact that we were moving forward with the cookbook as I made myself a coffee. Plus, I shared a few highlights from my conversation with Greer.

Dixie was headed out to pick up some supplies, and I decided to take advantage of the quiet in the office to buckle down on getting those contracts together.

I'd no sooner settled myself at my desk than the bell at the front door dinged. We hardly ever had business walk in off the street, so I figured it was probably one of the other merchants on the square. Likely Disco looking for "samples" or Tina with some additional gossip. I found myself hoping for Tina, as she might have had some insight into what was happening with the murder investigation.

"Hello," I called. Taking my coffee with me, I headed out to the front.

It was even better than Tina, as far as a murder investigation update went. It was Sheriff Terry.

I set my mug of coffee down and went back to the kitchen for one for him. By the time I'd returned, he was seated on one of the stools at our reception counter.

"Thanks." He took a sip and set the mug down.

I had a ton of questions, but I resisted. He was definitely here for a reason, so I'd hold off until he'd had his say.

"No sample cookies or muffins today?" Sometimes, the sheriff was as bad as Disco.

"No, Dixie took the leftover cookies to the chamber office before she left for the day. I'm so sorry because they were amazing." I was messing with him about the cookies because I knew his weakness, but I also knew he wanted to ask whether Dixie was around and was holding back. Theirs was a complicated attraction.

"Shoot." His face fell.

Probably disappointment on both counts.

"Okay, there might be a cookie or two left." Heading back to my office, I grabbed a napkin and lifted a couple of cranberry chocolate chip cookies from the container Dixie had left behind for me to take home. The sheriff would appreciate them, and my thighs would thank me for not taking them home to snack on.

Handing them to Sheriff Terry, I pulled up a stool. "What's up? I bet you didn't just come by for coffee and cookies."

He grinned. "No, but thanks."

"You're welcome." I waited.

Setting aside his cookies, his face got serious. "I haven't seen the coroner's report yet, and as this is a murder investigation, the DCI will soon step in to help. But clearly, Marla Mercer was stabbed."

"Right. The image of that bread knife sticking out of her back is seared into my brain. I assume you took it as evidence. So that crazy big knife that Mame had could not have been the murder weapon, right?"

"Right," he agreed. "But the knife that was used to kill Marla, as near as we can tell, isn't from the historical society's kitchen. It's different. And the knife that Mame had on her matches the design. Like it's from the same set."

"Wow." I thought about the implications. And tried to remember where Mame had come from when she burst in on the day of the murder. "I guess that looks bad. Do you think she could have …" I couldn't even finish the question.

The sheriff took advantage of my ruminating to take another bite of cookie and a sip of coffee.

"I don't see it." No doubt the evidence made Mame look bad, but why?

"I don't either, but Marla left everything to her. With Marla dead, she inherits everything." He finished off the cookie and leaned back.

"From what Greer was telling me, it amounts to quite a lot." Even with the money as a motive, I was still having trouble picturing Mame as Marla's killer. She seemed genuinely broken up over Marla's death. Sure, people can fake grief, but I didn't think Mame had it in her.

"Have you charged her?" I asked.

"No. She says she was at the elementary school where she helps with the school lunch program." He sighed and took another sip of his coffee. "But it was early and no one else saw her. We're checking the school's security cameras."

"What does she say about the knife?"

"She claims that it was Marla's and that she gave it to her. We're working on a warrant to search Marla's house and the cottage where Mame lives."

"It just doesn't make sense to me." I took a drink of coffee. "Why would she kill her best friend?"

"Stranger things have happened. But for what it's worth, everyone I've talked to says the same thing." He shrugged.

"Mame seemed to think there was some animosity toward Marla from some of the board members. But when I was at the historical society board meeting earlier—which was near chaos, by the way—that didn't seem to be the case; the board members seemed, like everyone else, baffled by who would want to kill Marla."

The bell over the door dinged again, and I was surprised to see Zac, the skateboarding kid who had been in with Hirsh's YAP group.

The kid didn't have much of a poker face. He clearly had not expected Sheriff Terry. I could see he wanted to turn around and go right back out the door. But to his credit, he didn't.

Sheriff Terry stood.

Now, Terry was tall and sort of nice-looking in a boy-next-door way, but when he was in full uniform with his badge, belt with flashlight, baton, and gun, I could see how he might seem intimidating. Especially if you were fifteen.

"I don't know if you two have met." I smiled, thinking if

they hadn't, that was probably a good thing. "Zac, this is Sheriff Griffin, and, Sheriff, this is Zac."

"Great to meet you." Terry reached out to shake Zac's hand. "I was getting ready to take off."

Zac hesitated for a few seconds but finally held out his hand. "Nice to meet you."

"Thanks for the coffee and cookies, Sugar." Sheriff Terry nodded at me and then turned to Zac.

"Stay off the sidewalk." He clapped a hand on Zac's shoulder.

The kid took a step back. "Yes, sir," he replied.

Was it my imagination, or was Zach a little jumpy? I waited until the sheriff had gone before I asked, "What brings you here?"

He shifted from foot to foot, and his curly, dark hair fell forward on his forehead. "Hirsh said I should come to talk to his sister or you."

"Dixie's not here right now, but you can talk to me." I indicated the stool the sheriff had recently vacated. "Would you like to sit?"

"Nah, that's okay." He continued to bounce from one side to the other, holding his skateboard under his arm. "I'm good."

There was a pause. The poor kid was incredibly nervous.

"What did you want to talk to us about?"

"Oh, right." He gave a short laugh. "I forgot. Okay, we wanted to ask if we could put a donation jar in your shop. You know, so people can put money in it to give to the skate park fund."

"I don't see any problem with that." I was glad he'd finally gotten his question out. "We don't get a lot of foot traffic, so I'm not sure it will take in a lot, but you're welcome to put one here."

"That's great. Any amount will help. Thank you so much." His words spilled out, and he was already headed for the door.

"Someone will bring you a jar," he said over his shoulder.

"Okay," I called, glad Hirsh was working with these kids.

I watched as he exited.

Once outside, he looked both ways before sliding his board on the sidewalk. Then, in one fluid motion, he landed his foot on the board and pushed off.

I shook my head.

He was lucky Sheriff Terry wasn't still around.

6

When I finally packed up my stuff and headed home, it felt like it had been more than one day since I started out that morning at the wacky St. Ignatius Historical Society board meeting. Between what I'd learned at the meeting, from Greer and the sheriff, and then from the awkward skateboarder, my head was full.

My stomach was not, though, and I had contracts to get done, so I hoped for an uneventful, no-one-at-my-door kind of evening.

That was not to be.

No sooner had I carted my purse and my bag filled with all the work I hadn't gotten done at the office in the house than there was pounding on the front door.

It had to be Mrs. Pickett. Everyone else used my in-perfect-working-order doorbell.

Ernest meowed, leaned against my legs, and looked up at me with a "Are you going to get that?" stare.

"Do I have to?" I asked.

His tail flip and subsequent collapse on the floor said, "You probably do, but don't take too long, as I am clearly on the verge of starvation."

So much drama.

I reluctantly moved to the door and opened it.

"Hello." As I'd suspected, it was my neighbor. I hoped she didn't want to come in again. That had been a major shocker, and I hadn't come up with any better coping skills since that visit. She was sporting a slightly different version of her previous outfit, with a flowered housedress under her house-coat. And though her hair wasn't in curlers, I didn't think she'd combed out the curls from yesterday, as they were still in such tight rolls that it looked like she had sausages on her head.

"They arrested Mame," she barked.

"No, they didn't," I corrected. "They took her to the county sheriff's office for questioning."

"She wasn't able to leave," she countered. "That sounds like arrested to me."

"I'm sure she always could have left, but they had questions for her and she agreed to go with the sheriff and answer them. She's home now, isn't she?"

"Yes." She nodded, the gray sausage curls bouncing. "But she was in jail for a while."

"Actually, I don't think so." I tried to be patient, as she was even more agitated than usual, but she needed to know that, though I was sure the experience was traumatic, there was a long way to go from being questioned to being arrested for murder. "You see—"

"What are you going to do about it?" she interrupted, her bony finger just inches from my nose.

I sighed.

Well, let's think about this.

In my mind, the sheriff took a very reasonable approach.

Oh, and I don't work for you.

And another thing, by the way, your niece brought a very large knife to my house.

I didn't say any of that. At this point, she was so distraught that I was a little worried about her. And also slightly worried about myself. Although Mrs. Pickett was not my favorite person in the world, I didn't wish her any ill will.

I sure didn't want her to have a heart attack on my front step.

But I also did not want her to hurt me.

"There are several other people they are talking to as well." I backed up a little in case she decided to get physical. "I don't think your niece has anything to worry about."

"Easy for you to say." She turned and stomped her way back to her house.

Stepping back and closing the door, I picked up my phone from the table inside the entry where I'd left it. I had a text.

Please don't let it be my mother.

Cate Sugarbaker Calloway was notorious for communicating with fifty texts when a five-minute phone call would have been easier. I could not deal with whatever first world problem she was having right now.

It was Dixie. *Are you home?*

Yes.

Great. I'm stopping by.

I sent her a thumbs-up and moved my work bag and the files I'd brought home to the living room. I feared I was not going to get those contracts done without having a very late night.

Ernest was still waiting, though impatiently, in the hallway, his tail flicking back and forth. I headed to the kitchen to get kitty kibble in his dish and fresh water in his bowl before I was in serious trouble with my housemate.

No sooner had I finished than my doorbell rang. "Come in," I called, completing my feline-directed duties and heading to the front door.

Dixie's hands were full, and I moved to grab one of the bags she was holding.

"I brought food." She headed toward the kitchen with the rest.

"Oh, bless you." I sniffed the bag I was holding and followed her to the kitchen. Whatever it was, it smelled amazing. Maybe something Italian? "You must be psychic. I didn't know what I was going to eat, and I think I may have skipped lunch. Well, except for that amazing homemade bread that Greer gave me. We had some butter at the office. It was delicious. We should get her recipe for the bread book."

Dixie rolled her eyes. "I'm sure it was good but definitely not a decent lunch." She began unpacking the bags. "I had this recipe for white lasagna I'd been wanting to try, and the directions said it was for four people. I thought, 'Okay, good. I'll have it tonight and then I can eat the leftovers another night. Maybe freeze some of it.'"

She turned to the oven and set it to preheat. "They must have meant forty people. Even with freezing some, I'll be eating lasagna for weeks. So I'm bringing part of it to you. We'll need to reheat it."

"Perfect." I removed Ernest from the countertop, as he had apparently smelled food and been sure that at least some of what Dixie had brought was for him. "Couldn't we just microwave it to save time?"

She stopped what she was doing and gave me a look. It had always been clear that Dixie was the food talent part of our team. Though I thought I had a healthy appreciation for good food, I'd apparently crossed a line with the microwave suggestion.

"Okay," I held my hands up in surrender. "I'll get the plates and find us a wine."

Thanks to my mother's good taste, I had some very nice wine glasses, and thanks to my own good taste, I had a modest but nice selection of wines. I picked out a Riesling since it appeared to be a white sauce lasagna and showed the wine to the chef for approval.

"You know better than I do what goes." She slid the pan of pasta into the now-warm oven and began slicing a crusty Italian bread she'd brought along. "Please tell me you have some good olive oil in your pantry."

"On it." Of course I did. I'm not a complete heathen. And though I didn't cook much, I did make a mean oil and vinegar salad dressing.

Handing over the olive oil, I cleared the table of my work things, poured us each a glass of wine, and set out plates.

"The lasagna only needs fifteen to twenty minutes to warm it since it's already cooked and hasn't had time to cool." Dixie placed the bread in a basket and put small plates of olive oil sprinkled with parmesan on the table. "We can start with the bread."

While we nibbled, I filled her in on the historical society board meeting, what Greer had said about the board members, and the few details the sheriff had shared about Mame.

"I gave Sheriff Terry cookies and coffee, but I think he was hoping you'd be there." I paused and waited for a reaction.

"Oh?" She didn't take the bait, but the blush said everything.

Those two hardheads.

I wasn't sure what it was going to take to get them to put aside the past and admit to the spark between them that was apparent to everyone else.

The oven timer dinged, and Dixie reached for oven mitts to take out the bubbly, cheesy pasta. I found a spatula, and we dished up a serving for each of us. We were about to dig in when my doorbell rang.

Please don't let it be Mrs. Pickett again.

She would have knocked though, right?

When I opened the door, I was shocked to see Mame Reinhart standing there.

"Can I come in?" She was still clutching her huge handbag, and I sent up a quick prayer that the sheriff's department had kept her knife even if they hadn't kept her.

"Sure." I held open the door.

"What's that smell?" Mame lifted her head and inhaled.

"It's lasagna." Dixie had come from the kitchen to see who it was. "Have you eaten? There's plenty."

"I haven't." Mame stepped in further, her nose in the air as if following the smells.

I gave Dixie a "What are you doing?" look—which she ignored.

"Well, come on in. Sugar and I were about to sit down." She waved a hand at the table.

Shaking my head, I grabbed another plate from the cupboard and set a third place at the table.

Okay, it was a good chance to ask Mame some questions, and I was sure that's what Dixie was thinking.

"Wow, that looks so good." Mame settled in and scooted up her chair, but I noticed she was keeping her bag by her side.

Not that I was seriously worried that she'd stopped by to kill us. But after the other night, I was a little bit on edge. Mame, on the other hand, seemed much less nervous than she'd been.

"Oh my gosh, this is so good," she mumbled, her mouth still full after the first bite. "Where did you get it?" She shoveled in another bite.

"Dixie made it," I explained, waiting for her to pause so I could ask what was really bugging me. "I'll bet you stopped by for a reason. Was there something you wanted to talk to me about?"

"I wanted to say sorry about the other night. I was so wound up with the people harassing me and that deputy telling me they thought I had something to do with Marla dying. I guess I acted kind of crazy. But I got it all straightened out with the sheriff." The words came out in a rush.

I thought it was mostly because she wanted to get the apology off her chest and partly because she wanted to get back to Dixie's lasagna.

"No need to apologize." I reached for my plate.

There was a brief silence as we all dug into the cheesy pasta. I grabbed a piece of the bread to mop up the sauce on my plate, not wanting to waste any of the goodness.

"How are you doing?" Dixie asked Mame.

"It's hard." She paused midbite. "Though we weren't roommates or anything. You know, with me living in the carriage house. But we saw each other most every day. Because neither of us had close family left, we relied on each other a lot." She took a deep breath and set her fork down.

"You have your aunt though, right?" I inclined my head in the direction of Mrs. Pickett's house and reached for the basket of bread again. Then, thinking better of that idea, I pushed the bread toward Dixie. Out of my reach.

"Yeah." Mame picked up herfork. "We actually aren't very close."

"I know she's worried about you." Maybe they weren't close, but Mrs. Pickett had sure seemed emotionally invested when she'd read me the riot act about Mame's trip to the sheriff's office.

"I'm fine. I just wish they would find whoever did this to Marla." She reached for the bread.

"Have you been over to her house?" Dixie asked.

"I've been taking in her mail and watering her plants. That's what I was doing when that skinny deputy said they thought I had something to do with … you know."

"But now they don't, right?" I tried to be reassuring without giving away what the sheriff had shared with me.

"I told them I was at the school, but nobody else was there. I go in early."

"But the school's security cameras should back you up, right?" That's what Sheriff Terry had said.

"I guess so." She didn't seem too reassured. "Too bad they don't have security cameras out at the historical complex. Then they could figure out who killed Marla." Her voice caught, and a tear slipped down her cheek. Her sense of loss was palpable.

Dixie and I looked at each other.

Guilt hit me like a punch to the stomach. How thoughtless had we been questioning her like it was some murder mystery dinner? She'd lost a friend. By all appearances, a best friend. Maybe her only friend.

And then, to top it off, there'd been no time for her to

grieve. She'd been questioned as if she had something to do with her friend's death.

"I'm so sorry for what you're going through." I reached over and laid my hand on her wrist.

"Do you know about services for Marla?" Dixie asked.

"That's one of the things I was trying to find at her house when I was over there. Marla was so organized. I know she had a file with what she wanted. She showed it to me one time. But it's hard to go over there."

"I'm sure it is difficult." Dixie stood and began picking up dishes. "Is there someone that can go with you?"

"Not really." Mame screwed up her face thinking about it. "The sheriff said the autopsy may take a while, so I guess I've got time."

We made short work of clearing the dishes, and Dixie put together a to-go bag for Mame with some of the lasagna and a couple of slices of the bread.

Plodding slowly to where she'd parked her car on the street, Mame carted her big purse and the bag with food.

I noticed she hadn't mentioned stopping in to see her aunt next door.

"Let us know if you need anything," I called as she got in. Then I watched until she pulled away.

At that moment, a car that had been parked farther down the street a ways started up and drove off as well.

And for the first time, I wondered whether it was safe for Mame to be staying in the carriage house alone with a murderer at large.

7

*E*arly the next morning, I was back at the Jameson County Historical Complex. I hoped someone was around for me to leave the cookbook contract with so it could be signed and we could get going on the cookbook project.

I should have asked more questions about the process when I'd been there for the board meeting. Someone, I assumed Lewis Brimley, as the new chair, needed to sign before we could get started. The board met only once a month, and if we waited until the next meeting, the delay would really mess with their timeline.

I stopped at the front office in the main building and asked the two women at the desk whether Lewis was around or whether they could provide a phone number for him. As they were discussing whether it was okay to give out his number, Racine walked in.

"Hi, Sugar." She was in blue jeans and a wool sweater, not the pioneer dress she'd always been wearing when I'd seen her before. Somehow, the modern dress made her look younger. "By the way, love your dress." She pointed.

"Thanks." I had pulled a favorite navy polka dot shift out of my closet this morning and then decided it wasn't warm enough to wear on its own. Adding a soft denim jacket had helped. "And the best feature of all: it has pockets." I demonstrated by reaching into the deep pockets on each side.

"I adore pockets." She grinned. "Are you looking for Lewis?"

"I am. I need to get this contract to him but realized I didn't have his phone number." I held up the paperwork.

"Oh, he's over at the farmhouse if you want to give it to him." She pointed in the direction of the low white building.

"Maybe you could give it to him when you see him?"

"I would, but I have a tour starting in a few minutes," she said. "And I need to get changed."

I'd thought about doing the tour before, and it would be good to do it now with the cookbook project beginning. It would not only be interesting but also spark some ideas.

"Are the tours walk-in? Or something that has to be scheduled?" I asked. "I couldn't join today, but it might help me get a feel for what we want to do with the design of the cookbook."

"Oh, they have to be scheduled. I don't do them every day, and I like to have at least ten people," she explained. "Are you interested? I could let you know when I have room in a group."

"I am interested. That would be great." I slipped the papers under my arm.

"Leave your phone number or email, and I'll let you know." She waved a hand toward the reception desk. "You can go on over to the farmhouse if you want. Lewis has been going through papers and, I imagine, could use a break."

I really needed to get back to the office, but it did seem like a great opportunity to chat with the new chair without all the chaos of a board meeting. Maybe I could get an idea of when he might be ready to share some of the recipes Marla had set aside for possible inclusion.

I left my phone number and email with the two women at the desk and set off across the complex to the farmhouse. I was a little surprised the space was already being used again, but the crime scene techs must have finished their work. As I walked around the buildings, I was once again struck by the beauty of the grounds. The big trees were majestic. The lawn and hedges were groomed to perfection.

I was glad my yard was much smaller in comparison. Between the mowing and the leaf raking, it was an undertaking. And heaven forbid that I didn't get to it straight away. Mrs. Pickett would be leaving me pointed reminders for sure.

I went around to the back, like I'd done on the morning I'd found Marla, and tapped on the door. I could see Lewis looking through papers at the counter island inside. No power tie today, but he was still dapper in chinos and a tan sports jacket. When he didn't look up, I knocked a little louder, and this time, he raised his head. I waved, and he smiled as he got to his feet and came to the door.

"Hello, Sugar," he said as he opened the door. "What brings you here?"

Stepping inside, I explained the contract and that I didn't have his number.

"Well, let's remedy that." He picked up his cell phone from the counter. "I'll give you mine, and I probably should get yours."

We exchanged numbers, and I handed him the contract. "You already have the proposal I gave Marla. That's what the board approved, and the terms of the contract are not any different. It lays out deadlines and approvals. Also, I wanted to make sure that we're clear on when we'll get the recipes from you and who will be approving the proofs of the cookbook."

"That would be me on the approval." He tapped his chest. "As far as the recipes, you can see that I have quite a lot of papers and things to go through here. Sadly, Marla was not very organized."

That wasn't what Mame had said, nor was it what I'd noticed, but who knew? Maybe there'd been something going on in her life that no one knew about.

"If you need help culling through potential recipes, we would be happy to help you with that." I picked up one of the recipes on the counter. It was handwritten on a piece of lined paper.

"I don't think that will be necessary." Lewis plucked it from my fingers and put it back in the proper pile. "It's important that these historic records be handled properly."

Okay, so Marla had probably been very organized but maybe not organized enough for Lewis. Dixie and I found that usually, our clients did need some help going through recipe selections. It could be overwhelming to decide on and keep a variety of recipes but not go overboard.

"Sometimes clients need help with narrowing the options," I explained. "The quote includes the number of pages we've agreed upon, and more recipes means more pages, which drives up the cost."

"Ah, I see." He paused. "Did Marla give you any papers or recipes before?"

"No, we only had preliminary discussions about what types of breads were or were not to be included." Eying Lewis's stacks, I saw another recipe I wanted to look at but resisted.

"And what were those types of breads?" Lewis smiled but laid his hand on top of one of the piles, as if he were afraid I'd mess up his system.

Ah, so that was going to be the challenge of this project. Lewis was a details person and clearly on the controlling side. Probably an accountant in a previous life. No worries; I'd dealt with his kind when I'd worked in the corporate world.

"Here's the list." I pulled a copy of the proposal from my folder. "Traditional breads, sweet breads, rolls and muffins, and family favorites."

"Hmm." He perused the list.

"I could help you sort—"

"No," he interrupted. "That won't be necessary. But this is helpful."

"Would you like to schedule some weekly check-ins?" I asked. Sometimes, the best way to prevent problems was to stay in front of them. I could see it might prove difficult to get the materials we would need from him if he got caught in a cycle of endless sorting. "I can keep you up to date on our progress, and you can share your decisions."

"Yes." Lewis smiled. "That might be a good idea."

We agreed on some dates and times, Lewis signed the contract, and then I headed back to my car. As I was placing my bag in the backseat, I noticed Racine and Zac, the skate-boarder, in conversation under one of the big maple trees.

It surprised me because I thought she'd said she had a tour and she still hadn't changed into her costume.

Maybe she didn't want to deal with Lewis and so had made up an excuse. But I wondered what the connection between her and Zac was. Probably not a romantic one because even though Racine was looking younger today, I thought she was still probably older than Zac.

I shrugged and got into Big Blue.

I had my work cut out for me trying to get Lewis to turn loose of his iron control of the historic recipes. Hopefully, the weekly meetings would keep things moving.

In the meantime, I was heading back to the office for some intense work on the *Tasty Notes Cookbook* for the high school band boosters, a big cup of coffee, and—fingers crossed—a tempting treat from Dixie's kitchen.

And the biggest treat of all, Max was stopping by to go over the layout and photos for the band booster cookbook.

8

When I came in the back door of the shop, I could smell something delicious baking and hear voices out front. Dropping my bags in my office and slipping my cell phone into my skirt pocket, I detoured through the kitchen to grab a cup of coffee and then headed toward the conversation.

Dixie was seated at the counter, still wearing her flour-splotched bright-blue apron over her jeans and navy sweatshirt. A strand of red hair slipped from the confines of her messy bun as she tipped her head back and took a swig of her standard morning glass of milk. Tina Martin, resplendent in today's fall-themed outfit of chocolate-brown pants and a burnt-orange sweater, was munching on one of Dixie's blonde brownies.

So that's what I smelled.

I did a quick U-turn. No way was I going to watch Tina nibble that treat to death in tiny bites. Not without a brownie of my own. I mean, have you ever had one of those crazy good blondies? Soft and decadent with butter and brown sugar and scattered chocolate clips. It's like the best part of a chocolate chip cookie. I picked up some napkins and plopped a blondie onto one.

OMG, the brownies were still warm.

Joining Dixie and Tina, I settled on a stool, tucking my skirt around my legs. It sounded like another discussion about Dino Diner. Only this time, Tina wasn't even pretending to keep any secrets. As I got closer, I noted Tina's coordinated look today included more than simply a matching manicure. Her blond hair was shot through with a streak of orange on one side.

"What?" Distracted by Tina's hair, I'd missed Dixie talking to me.

"Tina was sharing some news about the visit from that reality diner food guy," she repeated.

"Dino." Tina supplied. "I heard that he might be in town with his 'scouts' to make plans for when they film the segment." She took a teensy bite. "So exciting."

In rebellion against her dainty control and to avoid the comment I wanted to make, I took a huge bite of my brownie. "Hmm." I nodded.

"Well, I'd better be going." Tina put her half-eaten brownie down on one of the napkins and turned to leave.

Is the woman actually going to leave half of a blondie behind?

"How did it go at the historical society, Sugar?" Dixie asked. "You have some …" She pointed to the side of her mouth.

Chocolate on my face? Don't care.

Picking up a napkin, I wiped my mouth anyway.

"Other side." Dixie pointed and turned to gather up all the items on the counter.

Tina stopped in her tracks. "Historical society? Isn't that where that poor woman was stabbed?"

"Sugar found her." Dixie was cleaning up and had missed my "Please don't throw me under the bus" glare.

"You did!" Tina gasped and returned to the counter. "How did I not know that? What were you doing there, anyway?"

"We're working on a bread cookbook for the historical society," I explained, hoping that might be boring enough for her to let it go. But it just wasn't in her DNA to drop it.

"What's the deal? Do they think it was the Cash Burglar?" She leaned in.

"The what?" Dixie asked.

I had no idea what she was talking about either.

She leaned her elbows on the counter and lowered her voice. "There have been all these break-ins around town, and the guy only takes whatever cash there is to be had. No jewelry, no electronics. He doesn't mess anything up. Grabs the cash and goes."

"I hadn't heard anything about the break-ins." I looked at Dixie, and she shook her head. "Is it just homes?"

"No, not homes, mostly businesses. Small ones that have petty cash on hand."

"So not a large amount of money." I didn't think there would be any reason for the historical society to have cash. Or at least not at the farmhouse. But if this had been going on, surely Sheriff Terry was considering the possibility of a break-in there.

"If it's petty cash, it's probably not much from each place, but I imagine that it adds up." Dixie continued wiping down the counter.

"You said 'he.' Do they know it's a he?" I asked.

"Not sure, but it must be somebody pretty small because

they always come in through a window." Tina straightened. "Maybe the lady that was killed surprised the Cash Burglar and he stabbed her."

"Could be." I still thought the intruder theory sounded kind of far-fetched but found it more reasonable than the idea that Mame had killed her best friend.

"If you keep any cash here, I'd be locking it up if I were you," she said over her shoulder as she went out the door.

"How did we not know about this Cash Burglar?" I shook my head and headed to the back for more coffee.

"I would have thought there would've been a mention on the merchants' association email loop or at the last meeting." Dixie followed me to the kitchen area.

I filled Dixie in on my conversation with Lewis and the fact that he seemed to want to micromanage the recipe selection.

"I can see that." She sat down and took another swig of her milk. "You know he's got an office nearby, right?"

"No, I don't know anything about him." I poured a fresh cup of coffee. "All my dealings were with Marla."

"He's not on the square, but his office is over on Greenwood, down by the fire station. I guess St. Ignatius history must be a hobby. Or else, why volunteer on the historical society board, right? But professionally, he's a tax guy."

"Bingo! Called it." I had refilled my cup but was debating eating half a brownie with the rest of my coffee. "When he was so hyper about me touching his piles of papers and recipes, I thought to myself, 'Probably an accountant in a former life.'"

"I don't know if it's exactly 'former.' I think he still does people's taxes. Maybe not as many as he used to but still quite a few."

"Okay, so we've got his 'number,' so to speak." I made quotation marks with my fingers, entertained by my own pun. "And we know how to deal with those spreadsheet types."

"I'll let you do that, funny lady." Dixie smiled. "I'll stick to the recipe testing parts of this project."

She took her glass and headed back to the kitchen. I unpacked the contract stuff from my bag and settled in to put the finishing touches on the next one up.

An hour later, when I heard a cheerful "hello" from the back door, I was happy for the interruption.

Max came through carrying his photo portfolio. "I hope it's okay I parked in the back. The parking on the square is packed today. Is there something going on that I missed hearing about?"

"If there is, I missed it too. Although my batting average isn't great on local news today." I stood and stretched. "Do you want to work at the counter out front? There's more space to spread out."

"That would be great." He looked at my desk. "Not a lot of room here."

"Hey, it's been busy." I had to admit my office was in more disarray than usual. The juggling of four projects at the same time might have been hitting the limit of what we could manage all at once.

"Wasn't a criticism at all." Max chuckled as he stepped back into the hallway. "Just an observation."

I stopped by the kitchen and warmed up my coffee, as it had gotten cold. "Max is here. Do you want to take a look at the photos?"

"Love to." Dixie put a towel over the bowl she had been working with. "Give me a minute to wash my hands, and I'll join you."

"Max, you do want coffee or anything?" I asked.

"Thanks, but no." He'd already begun laying photos out on the counter.

I walked around looking at what he'd captured. Although I'd worked with professional food photographers before I'd parted ways with Mammoth Publishing, Max's capabilities always amazed me.

He'd been a photojournalist before an injury changed his career path, and he had never done any culinary photography before working with us. But I'd come to the conclusion that his lack of experience in that area was perhaps less disadvantage and more advantage. Storytelling with photos was his superpower, so while his photos showcased the dish, they also pulled in the context of the story behind the recipe. Perfect for the type of cookbook that is, most of all, a collection of recipes representing a group or an effort.

"I love how this is coming together." I stepped around to stand beside him. "This is one of my favorites." I pointed to a photo of a big batch of homemade Crunch & Munch. It had been taken from above the bowl and showed teenaged hands reaching in from each direction.

Dixie joined us and also circled the counter, checking out the photos. "Oh, this is going to be hard, isn't it?"

"It is." I sighed.

"How many do we have room for?" She reached out and pulled a photo forward.

I opened the folder, which included a mock-up of the layout from Liz, our graphic designer. "We have six sections. So larger photos for those section breaks and then room to highlight two recipes in each section with smaller photos."

We culled a handful of favorites and moved them to the

end of the counter. This could all have been done online, but we'd used this process since the beginning and it worked for us. I wasn't sure I'd have the same ability to visualize the photos in a book if I did it online.

"You need four more. And you may want to review how those you've picked go together as far as perspective and angle are concerned." Max took a look at what we'd selected so far and then stepped back. "I can edit, of course, but to get the seamless element we're looking for, you'll want a blend of symmetry and contrast."

Dixie and I looked at him and back at the photos.

I was the sales and project manager part of the business. Dixie was the blue-ribbon baker and food expert. We probably needed to bring Liz in on the photo selection process, as she spoke Max's language, but she didn't live in town. And she'd been clear she'd work with us as long as she didn't have to travel.

Just then, the bell over the door dinged, and Sheriff Terry stepped in. He was in full uniform, which always made the situation feel more serious. He shook hands with Max, and they exchanged greetings. Max explained what we were doing as Dixie and I continued looking through the remaining photos.

"I can come back if it's a bad time." The sheriff moved toward the counter. He was tall enough to see over my shoulder. He pointed at a photo of mouthwatering barbecued wings. "Nice."

That was one of the photos I'd been considering. In fact, after staring at it for the last five minutes, I was now considering having barbeque for lunch.

"We could definitely use a break," I said, stepping to the other side to retrieve my coffee.

Dixie disappeared to the back and then returned shortly with the coffee pot, cups, and a few of the remaining brownies on a plate.

I cleared a spot safely away from the photos.

Both Sheriff Terry and Max reached out for a cup and a brownie.

Dixie poured. "So what brings you by?"

The sheriff took a sip of coffee. "I stopped by to tell you the access control system they use to log entry to the school confirmed Mame's whereabouts on the morning Marla Mercer was killed."

"That's good." I was glad Mame had been cleared and also hoped that meant Mrs. Pickett was done harassing me. At least about Mame, anyway.

"I guess she could've entered and climbed out a window at the school, then climbed back in in time for the janitor to see her an hour later, but I don't see that happening." The sheriff set his cup aside. "She is not a small woman."

"She is tall." Dixie slid out a stool and sat. "Any other leads?"

Sheriff Terry frowned. "We're looking at the potential that this could be related to some break-ins around town."

"But I wouldn't think the historical society would have much cash on hand, and those have been only cash thefts, right?" I asked.

He looked up. "How did you—"

"Tina Martin," I answered, taking a sip of my coffee.

Sheriff Terry shook his head. "We were trying to keep details under wraps, but that's obviously not possible in St. Ignatius."

"How many break-ins have there been?" I moved to the other side of the counter and pulled out a stool for myself.

"We've had eight." He rubbed his neck. "Which doesn't sound like many, but that's quite a few in a short period of time."

"All cash?" I asked.

"That's right, all cash and not a lot of cash. Mostly places where it's easy to find and not locked up at all."

"How did they get in?" Dixie stood.

"Well, again, this is St. Ignatius, right?" He wiped his face with his hand. "Some people in town aren't great about locking their doors. Others leave a key in an obvious place."

I looked at Dixie. A while back, we'd had a discussion about her leaving a key in the flowerpot behind the shop. Hopefully, she'd stopped doing that.

"And in other cases, the thief came in through a window," Sheriff Terry continued.

"I bet the historical society does have cash on hand but probably not in that building."

"Are you thinking the Cash Burglar broke in not expecting anyone to be there, and when they surprised Marla, there was a struggle?" I kept trying to remember whether it had looked like there might have been a struggle. I pictured some things on the floor—books and boxes, but they were stacked. It hadn't looked much different from the first time I'd been there.

"The 'Cash Burglar?'" The sheriff rolled his eyes and reached for another brownie.

Dixie gave him a look.

"What? I missed breakfast." He nabbed another one to make his point.

"They were even better when they were warm." I was going to have to skip lunch if I ate one more of those addictive treats. "That's what Tina said people are calling him," I explained. "Or her."

Max pulled out one of the stools and joined the group. "Sorry to be an armchair detective or ask the obvious, but were none of these break-ins caught on security cameras?"

"Not a single one." Sheriff Terry shook his head. "Clearly not someone passing through. They know the town, know the businesses, and know who keeps cash."

Max rubbed his chin. "That seems like a pretty big leap though, from petty theft to murder."

We were all silent for a few minutes.

My cell phone rang, breaking the spell.

9

Reaching into my pocket, I pulled out my cell phone and pressed it to my ear. I stepped away and looked at the caller ID but didn't recognize the number.

"Hello."

"Sugar?" the vaguely familiar female voice said.

"Yes," I replied.

"This is Mame. Mame Reinhart." Ah, that's why the voice sounded familiar.

"Hello, Mame." I could sense Sheriff Terry's gaze burning into the back of my head. I turned around and smiled at him, then swung back around to continue the call.

"You remember I told you I was kind of reluctant to go into Marla's house but I have been taking her mail in and stuff?"

"Right." The room behind me was still silent.

"Well, today, on her desk, I found some recipes and papers that look like they might have been for the historical society cookbook. I'll try and get them to you."

"Thanks, Mame. If you're going to be home, I could swing by and pick them up on my way home," I offered.

"That would be great." I could hear the relief in her voice.

We hung up, and I turned back to the room. "Mame found some recipes and things for the cookbook. I told her I'd pick them up." I looked to Sheriff Terry. "Any problem with that?"

"Where'd she find the papers?" he asked.

"On Marla's desk."

"We've been through her desk, so no worries there." He brushed the crumbs from his uniform and turned to go.

"Thank you for the breakfast." He grinned at Dixie, gave Max and me a wave, and was off.

Once Sheriff Terry was gone, Max stood. "Why don't we take out the photos you're not considering? Then it may be easier to narrow down those last few."

"Great idea." Dixie also got to her feet.

Once we had fewer photos to look at, we quickly came to a consensus on which ones we wanted to go with for the remaining recipes.

Max packed up his stuff as Dixie cleaned up our snack area.

Once Max left, I settled in at my desk in an attempt to get my head back into proposals for the new clients.

The rest of the day went by in a blur, with Dixie in the kitchen and me in the office. I was excited to see what Mame had found. To be honest, our content for the cookbook so far was a little sparse.

When I pulled into the driveway at Marla's home, I didn't see Mame's carriage house right away. The lot was long and deep, and the driveway went past the big house and stopped beside a park-like backyard. On the other side of the drive was a good-sized structure painted a soft gray with white trim like the main house.

I knew carriage houses were popular in the 18th and 19th centuries and located on the properties of larger homes. Back in the day, they were used for horse-drawn carriages and their equipment. Most have now been converted to other uses, such as garages, workshops, and home offices. Some larger ones, like this one where Mame lived, were made into guest houses or rental properties.

The large trees in the back were shading the house, and the setting sun was peeking through the leaves. It was beginning to get dark earlier, and though I mostly loved the change of seasons, early darkness was one of the things I did not like. Mame already had the lights on inside her place, but Marla's house stood tall and dark in the waning light.

Getting out and approaching the carriage house, I couldn't spot a doorbell. I knocked.

The door cracked open an inch, and Mame peered out.

"Just making sure it was you, Sugar." She opened the door wider. "I'm a little creeped out with a killer on the loose."

"Not to scare you, but you are kind of isolated back here." I looked around. "Have you thought about some security?"

"I've thought about getting one of those door cameras." She waved me in.

"That might be a good idea. We've been considering one for the shop." I stepped inside. "They're pretty easy to install, or I'm sure you could hire someone to hook it up."

Mame's decorating style seemed to be Victorian mixed with boho-chic and early chaos. And heavy on the chaos. There were some really nice Victorian pieces scattered throughout. The hall tree/bench looked like tiger oak, and I was certain one of the tables was an Eastlake. I could see the distinctive spindles and carvings of that style, but it was almost covered in piles of fabric.

"Do you sew?" I asked. "Or quilt?" As I moved farther into the living area, I could see more piles of fabric.

"I used to," she replied, moving a basket of yarn from the couch so I could sit. "Now I'm more into crocheting." She placed the basket by an armchair where I could see she'd laid down whatever it was she'd been working on. "I make dishcloths and pot holders. Little baby blankets for the hospital. You know, easy things."

"I'm afraid none of that is easy for me. I have no talent where those kinds of things are concerned." I sat down in the space she'd cleared on the couch. "Nor any cooking talent, for that matter. Thank goodness for Dixie."

"I make a mean apple pie." Mame picked up her crocheting and plopped down in her chair. "But that's the extent of my cooking skills. Marla was the better cook, and she always loved collecting recipes." She took up where she'd left off on what looked to be a red-and-white potholder. "Even when we were teenagers. I think maybe because when her mom died, she ended up taking over all the cooking for her dad. And then she ended up taking care of him when he got sick. She would try to find different things to encourage him to eat."

Her crochet hook was flying as fast as her words.

"How old was she when her mother died?" I hadn't realized all the history between the two friends.

"I believe she was ten." Her fingers continued to fly. "I was a little younger when I lost my parents. It was probably the fact we didn't have moms that brought us together as friends.

That kind of thing really stands out when it's Parents' Day at school or the rotation for homeroom mothers."

"That had to be hard." I knew a little bit about that myself. My dad hadn't been around when I was young, and my mom had usually been working. "You two were friends for a long time."

Mame nodded, her eyes filling with tears. "Almost like sisters."

"Oh, honey, I am so very sorry." I reached over and patted the arm of her chair. "If there's anything we can do to help, please let us know."

"Thanks." She sniffed, wiping the corner of her eye on her forearm.

I looked around for a tissue, but not knowing where to even look in all the piles, I finally reached into my bag for the packet I always kept there. I handed it to her, but there was a moment when I didn't think she would let go of her crochet hook long enough to take it.

Finally, she placed the yarn and hook on her lap.

"It's hard." She wiped her eyes with the tissue. "I'm having trouble even going into the house. I know that eventually, I'll have to do it and go through her things. There's no one else."

"Give yourself some time." I wasn't sure what the process was, but I was pretty sure there were some legal steps. "Have you heard from her attorney?"

"Yeah. He's that George McCormack on the square."

"And did he give you a timeline?"

"Sort of." She set the tissue aside and picked up her crocheting. "He said all the bills and things have to be paid, accounts closed, and such. But he said it's okay if I go in the house. You know, to take in mail, water plants, and straighten things up."

I could think of a few things that needed straightening up at Mame's place before she did anything like that at Marla's house.

"When you're ready to tackle going through things, if you need some help or moral support, you give me a call, okay?"

"Okay." She continued the looping of the bright yarn in and out of her hook. "I will."

"What was it you found that you thought might be related to the cookbook project?" I needed to get moving, or I was in for a severe scolding from Ernest when I got home.

She shifted and pulled a bag out from under her chair. "I found these and put them in a folder. I don't know if they're something for the cookbook, because she has lots of recipes, but these were on her table, not with her own recipes."

I flipped through the items in the folder. They did seem to be older recipes, but there weren't any notes to give me context.

"I'm not sure because I don't yet have the rest of the material from Lewis Brimley. But once I do, maybe I can tell. If you don't mind, I'll keep them until then."

"Sure, that's fine." She waved a hand. "Why don't you have the stuff from Lewis?"

"He wanted to go through it first," I explained.

"He's a control freak, that one." She pushed the bag back under her chair. "Came over and wanted to know if I had any historical society papers. I said no, but then he wanted to look over at the house. I said no. She always kept historical society papers in her briefcase, which I bet the sheriff has."

"I'll bet you're right. Thank you for this." I tapped the folder. "I appreciate it."

"You're welcome." Mame yawned.

I knew she got up early to get to the school before the

elementary kids arrived for breakfast. "I'd better be going." I tucked the folder under my arm and picked up my purse.

Mame walked outside with me, and we said goodbye. I waited until she was back inside and I heard her flip the lock before I headed to my car.

Backing out of the long driveway was a challenge. I used my rearview mirror, as well as my side mirrors, to try to stay on the drive and make sure I didn't damage any of the low greenery that lined the sides.

Almost there. I could see the edge of the curb in my mirror.

Easing backward, I shifted my gaze to the forward view and congratulated myself on how far I'd come without going off into the bushes or the yard.

Then I slammed on the brakes.

The hair on the back of my neck stood up.

There was a tall, thin man standing by the front window of Marla's house. I wouldn't have spotted him if it hadn't been for my headlights.

Grabbing my phone, I got out of the car.

"Hey!" I yelled. "What are you doing there? I am calling the police right now."

The man didn't move.

A thousand things went through my mind at once.

Was he watching and waiting for me to leave Mame's place? Is he the Cash Burglar taking advantage of the dark and an empty house? He must have seen me stop the car. What if he comes after me? What if he gets away? What is the response time for the sheriff's department?

I kept my eyes on him as I fumbled with my phone, figuring he might run and I would need to be able to tell the officer in which direction he'd gone.

I finally got 9-1-1 punched in my phone, and keeping my eyes on the intruder, I took a step back. Suddenly, the area was flooded with light. There must have been a front yard light with a motion detector, and either the burglar or I had set it off.

Still, he didn't move.

The dispatcher answered. "9-1-1, what's your emergency?" the brisk voice asked.

At that exact same moment, in the bright light, I could see that the figure I'd been watching was not a man but a colorfully dressed scarecrow staged as part of Marla's fall decorations.

Greer had nothing on Marla. Pumpkins and thatches of cornstalks were winding through baskets of flowers and a wreath of red and orange leaves. And a tall scarecrow was dressed in a checkered shirt and jaunty overalls.

Blowing out a breath, I was flooded with relief, and I laughed out loud.

"Hello, are you there? What is your emergency?" the voice on my phone barked.

"Oh, uh, so sorry. False alarm."

I jabbed the disconnect button and hurried back to my car.

Pulling into my driveway an hour later than my usual time to get home, I sat in the Jeep for a bit, still trying to calm myself down.

On edge much?

My jumpiness at Marla's had been silly. But there had been a murder, and according to Sheriff Terry, they had no real suspects.

The idea that it could have been someone who was breaking in when they'd surprised Marla made sense. And they could have struggled. But like Max had said, it's a big leap from committing several small cash-only thefts to killing someone. Still, it could have been that the person panicked and didn't necessarily mean to kill Marla.

Or it could have been something else entirely.

Taking a deep breath, I gathered my things and went inside to face my cat.

The next morning, I was still shaking my head at my foolishness and thanking my lucky stars that I hadn't told the 9-1-1 dispatcher about the "scary intruder." If I had, I would have had to explain to one of Sheriff Terry's deputies that what I'd thought was a criminal pulling off a B and E was a jaunty fall decoration.

When I arrived at the office, I could tell Dixie was already there and had been baking.

I filled Dixie in on the scarecrow incident, and I had to say, in my opinion, she laughed harder than was appropriate for a best friend.

"It's not that funny," I grouched, refilling my coffee.

"Pretty funny, though." She stopped working with the dough she had on the counter long enough to chuckle some more. "Would have been even funnier if you'd told them about 'Scary Guy.' You would have never lived it down in this town."

"I know." Again, Lady Luck had been with me. "Now that

I've completed the entertainment segment of the morning, I'm off to my fancy corner office to get some work done."

However, no sooner had I sat down in my chair than my cell phone rang.

It was Lewis Brimley from the historical society, and he had finished going through Marla's papers and notes. He was ready to hand off the recipes she'd already picked. I had to give him credit for how quickly he'd worked through everything. I'd been worried, as persnickety as he'd seemed, that it would take longer. Now that I knew he had an office nearby, I offered to pick up the recipes. He explained he wouldn't be at the office until around ten o'clock, so I said I'd stop by after that.

Spending time on the tearoom proposal and some mop-up on the pie shop contract took me most of the morning. Sipping coffee and nibbling on one of Dixie's leftover blondies made the work more pleasant. I was so glad she'd made a big batch. I looked up at the clock, noting it was ten on the nose.

It was a beautiful fall day. Lewis's office was close and I could use the exercise, so I decided to walk. I was not as color coordinated as Tina Martin usually was, but I had managed to assemble a semi-put-together look with a crisp white shirt, black leggings, and a longish black-and-gray plaid jacket. With the jacket, I should be warm enough for a short walk.

"I'm heading over to pick up the recipes from Lewis Brimley," I called to Dixie. "It's only a couple of blocks, right?"

She stuck her head out of the kitchen area. "Yep, down to the end of the block, toward Tressa's, and then turn right at the antique store and go one more block. You'll see it on your right."

"Got it. Right and then right." I smiled. Dixie knew better

than to give me north-south-east-west instructions, as I had no sense of direction at all. Absolutely none. If it weren't for my Jeep's GPS, I'd be lost more times than not.

Heading out the front door, I waved at Lark Travers, who was leaning forward into the big display window inside his shop, straightening the row of engagement rings. Jameson County Real Estate was next in line, but all I could see through their windows were bits and pieces of the reception area. The window was plastered with pictures of houses and farmsteads for sale. I didn't pause to look. I still held out hope that when Greer was ready to sell her house, she'd give me the first crack at it rather than listing it.

At the corner, I turned right and passed Auntie's Attic, the antique furniture store that took up the corner storefront. I loved to browse there, but there was no time for that now. Maybe on the way back. As I turned the corner and headed down the block, I spotted my destination. Lewis Brimley Tax Advisor was written in fancy gold letters on the window. I tried the door, and it was open, so I stepped inside.

There was no one at the reception desk, but the jangle of the bells attached to the door must have alerted Lewis because he called out, "Be right with you." He came out from the back carrying a steaming cup of coffee.

"Good morning," I said.

"Would you like some?" He lifted the cup in question.

"No, thanks." I shook my head. "I've already reached my morning limit. I stopped by to pick up the recipes."

"Yes." He opened a drawer and pulled out a folder. "Here you go."

I took the folder and opened it. "Do you know how many recipes you have in here?"

"There are eighteen and a half." He looked over his coffee cup at me.

"A half?" I raised a brow.

"There's one recipe Marla had in there that seems to be incomplete." He shook his head. "I don't know why she'd have half a recipe in the box, but I included it in case you know what the rest of it might be."

"I most likely don't, but maybe Dixie does." I shrugged. "She's the baker in our business." I almost mentioned the papers Mame had given me but stopped myself. If there was anything there I thought needed to be included, I'd bring it to him. But for sure, if I so much as mentioned the papers, Mr. Control Freak would want me to turn them over for his review.

"When can we expect to see a draft?" he asked.

"We're quite a few steps away from a draft," I explained, thinking to myself that the details were all in the contract he'd signed. "We'll review the recipes here and then see what gaps we have. I may need to ask you and the other board members for some additional material."

"No need to trouble the board." He waved a hand. "You can go through me for that."

"Thanks. I will." I turned to go, and as I did, I noticed two boxes on the edge of the reception desk, an antique-looking wooden one with brass fittings and a small gray metal one.

I turned back. "Do you keep cash here in your office?"

"Some. Why do you ask?"

I hesitated. Sheriff Terry hadn't asked us not to say anything. And the cat had been out of the bag once Tina had known about it anyway. "I guess there have been some break-ins around town involving cash."

"Really?" He looked shocked, so he must not have had occasion to talk with Tina. "Oh, dear."

"You may want to lock it up or at least make sure it's out of sight."

"Break-ins here on the square?"

"Not only here, as I understand it, but mostly small businesses, small amounts of cash."

"We've never had any problems in the past, but I'll take your advice." Lewis picked up the gray box and put it in a desk drawer. "Thanks for the tip."

I headed back to the shop, giving Auntie's Attic a pass. Maybe if I made great progress on the recipe sorting, I'd treat myself to some browsing later in the day.

When I walked through the front door of Sugar & Spice, Zac, the young skateboarder, was perched on one of the stools at the counter, munching on the leftover blondies from yesterday and talking with Dixie.

There goes my afternoon snack.

I was glad I'd had one with my morning coffee. It was just as well. I had no self-control when it came to those brownies, and with what I'd consumed yesterday, I probably needed to add a mile to my morning run.

Dixie looked up. "Zac dropped off the donation jar." She tapped a gallon-sized glass jar wrapped in a sign that said Support the Skate Park Project.

"Great." I eyed the jar as I joined them. "Do you have these at a lot of businesses?"

"Some," Zac said around his mouthful of brownie. "Most of the ones on the square have been supportive."

"It would be great if you could get a corporate donor," I mused. I wasn't sure how much a skate park cost, but I bet it was a lot. "There's a big skate park in Des Moines, isn't there?"

"Yeah, it's the largest in the US and brings in some pros." Zac perked up considerably. Now we were talking his language. "Those guys are sick."

"But a bit of a drive, right?" I was trying to gauge whether Zac was old enough to drive or not. Did someone have to drive the kids to the skate park?

"We're not talking about a USA Skateboarding-certified park here like in Des Moines. We need something local to practice our tricks. I just got my fakie frontside 180, and Gil—you met him the other day—he just got his revert, but we're getting better."

"Hmmm," I replied, looking over at Dixie.

She nodded. Though I was sure she understood no more of what Zac had said than I did.

Suddenly, Zac's phone buzzed. He pulled it out of his pocket and looked at it. "I'd better get going."

"Thanks for dropping off the donation jar." Dixie stood.

"Yeah, uhm. Thanks for letting us have it here." And with that, he grabbed his board and was out the door.

"I have no idea what he was saying about the 'fakie' something." Dixie shook her head.

"Me neither." I laughed. "But he's very enthusiastic about it."

"Yes, he is. I wish them well, but I'm not sure we need that big of a jar."

"I didn't want to say anything in front of Zac and spread more rumors about the thefts, but we'd probably better figure out a way to lock that up when we leave each day." I pointed at the big glass jar. "By the way, when I was at Lewis's office, I spotted a cash box sitting out and suggested he needed to secure it. He hadn't heard about the Cash Burglar, so apparently, Tina hadn't stopped by."

"I imagine it was more of a case of he's hardly ever at the office this time of year. Probably more so during tax season." Dixie wiped down the counter and picked up the now-empty brownie container. "We can probably lock it up in one of the cabinets."

"I don't know that we're going to raise much for the cause." I wished we could help more.

"We have so little foot traffic that it's hardly worthwhile."

"Let me take that." I held out my hand for the empty brownie container. "Though I'm still not going to forgive you for giving all the blondies to the kid."

She smiled. "He really liked them."

"Do you want to take a look at these recipes from Lewis?" Picking up the folder from Lewis, I handed it to Dixie. "I'm going to grab the batch from Mame. There's this first half of a recipe in what Lewis gave us. Maybe you can tell if there's anything in there that might be the rest of it."

"Okay." Dixie opened the folder and began looking through the contents.

I headed back to the office to grab the folder from Mame.

"Don't forget we have a merchants' association meeting this evening at six." Dixie reminded me.

I groaned.

THE ST. IGNATIUS MERCHANTS' ASSOCIATION MET IN THE BACK room of the Red Hen Diner monthly, and usually, at this time of year, the talk was all about the Fall Festival. It was one of my favorites of the town's celebrations and involved hayrack rides, hot apple cider, and pumpkin bowling, as well as a parade, a bonfire, and a corn maze. This meeting, however, was all abuzz with the pending arrival of Dino Diner and his visit, which would happen prior to the festival.

The mayor had been contacted by Dino's people and asked to keep the plans under his hat.

We already knew how that had gone. Someone—maybe Mayor Kirby—had let it slip to Tina, and now everyone around the square knew. And all their relatives and friends.

Dino was known for both his enthusiasm for diner food and his derision for what he determined to be "not cool." And while I loved everything the Red Hen served, I hoped Dino would too and wouldn't throw one of his ugly fits over the homey atmosphere. Toy George, the Red Hen's pint-sized proprietor, would not hesitate to take him on.

I'd tried to convince Dixie that we didn't both need to be at this meeting, but she was insistent that we did. And though I wasn't sure I had a lot to contribute, I was never one to turn down free pie.

I eased toward the table that held plated slices. I was after a cherry if they weren't already gone, but I had my second choice (apple) in mind if all the cherry had been scooped up.

My hand was reaching for the final slice of cherry pie just as another hand swooped in and grabbed it. I turned to scowl at the swiper and then smiled when I realized it was Dixie. I was pretty sure I could talk her out of it.

"Hand over the pie, and no one will get hurt." I held out my hand.

"I thought you said you were giving up desserts for a month." She smiled and held it aloft. Dixie is considerably taller than me. Heck, most everyone, excluding Toy, was taller than me.

"Why on earth would I say something like that?" I

continued to hold out my hand. "If I did say that, I must have been delusional."

"All right." Dixie handed over the plate and slipped a fork on it. "I like the lemon meringue better anyway."

"Did you hear the latest?" Tina Martin sidled up beside us and picked up a slice of banana cream pie, which I had to resist taking away from her.

I'd seen Tina eat pie before, and I was willing to bet she was going to eat only the bananas off the top and none of the good stuff. What a waste of an excellent piece of pie. No one who was going to eat only the garnish should be allowed to have it.

"No. What's the latest?" Dixie asked.

"Well …" Sure enough, Tina plucked a sliced banana right off the top of that slice of pie and popped it into her mouth. "They've released Mame Reinhart. I guess she's no longer a murder suspect."

"Why would she have killed Marla?" Dixie handed Tina a fork. "They were best friends."

"I guess." Tina used the fork to lift another banana slice. "But I've been told that Marla left everything to her. Her house, what's in it, everything. Isn't that a little odd?"

You know what's odd? Eating the bananas off the top of a pie.

"I don't see it." I turned away. Partly because I couldn't watch Tina pick at that wonderful pie any longer and partly because I hated to think that the jump-to-conclusions gossip had continued.

As I turned, I caught a glimpse of a short and stocky platinum-haired guy. He was hard to miss with that hair and his signature red shirt. Dino Dinelli, better known as Dino Diner.

He wouldn't remember me.

But as our eyes met from across the room, I could see that he did.

He looked like he might have been heading my way, but then Mayor Kirby took him by the arm and tugged him in another direction.

I slid my half-eaten cherry pie onto a table and left the room.

By the time I came back, Dino and the mayor were both gone and the meeting was in full swing. I slipped into a chair beside Dixie, and she gave me a look.

"Where did you disappear to?" she asked.

"Stepped outside for some fresh air." I fanned myself with one hand.

"Right." She raised a brow. "They're talking about the auction for the skate park fundraiser."

"Great." I settled in to listen.

I was going to have to deal with Dino eventually, but tonight was not the night.

11

The next morning, I arrived at the office before Dixie, which meant that no yummy baking smells greeted me. The shop felt a little on the cool side, and I was glad I'd opted for jeans and my fisherman knit sweater. Checking the thermostat, I reminded myself that the fall I loved so much also brought cooler temps. And obviously, with no baking happening to take the edge off, the morning chill seemed even cooler.

I started making coffee and wished I'd swung by the Red Hen and grabbed a blueberry muffin. I opened cupboards, looking for any leftovers, but didn't find a thing. It was maybe just as well; as my scale and step counter frequently reminded me, I needed to move more and knock off the sampling.

Once the coffee was ready, I poured a cup and took my mug out front. Unlocking the door, I wondered whether we should have had a security camera before now. We kept only a little cash on hand because none of our clients paid in cash. Or paid at the shop, for that matter. We invoiced them, and they paid via check or bank transfer. Easy-peasy.

In the shop, the only items we actually had for sale were surplus copies of the cookbooks we'd done. But since the books had been created for the groups who had hired us, we rarely sold a copy. And even then, most people paid with a credit card or an app.

I'd tried to get Dixie to do a cookbook with her award-winning recipes. I knew people would love that. And we'd have something to sell that showcased her talent and our product. But she wasn't convinced. Some of the blue-ribbon winners' recipes were featured in the Iowa State Fair cookbooks that the fair did each year. She had been in those and thought that was enough.

Musing about how far we'd come in the short time we'd been in business, I stared out the big plateglass window. Foot traffic was light, but then it usually was this time of day. Mostly other merchants from around the square or people headed to the Red Hen for breakfast. The courthouse in the center of the square wasn't open yet, but those who worked there were beginning to arrive.

Okay, enough dilly-dallying. Better get to work.

As I backed away from the window, I spotted Dino Dinelli outside. Checking out storefronts as he walked, he was sporting his usual black jeans and black T-shirt. He hesitated in front of the shop for a moment, eyeing the Sugar & Spice Cookbooks sign. Then he reached for the handle. The bell above the door dinged as he entered. I could feel my blood pressure tick up.

"What, no cluck?" he asked.

I eyed him steadily, not taking the bait. I sure wished I'd never unlocked that door and waited for Dixie's arrival instead.

"Please." I took a sip from my mug. "I've not had enough coffee to deal with your sarcasm so early."

"Quite a change from your posh corner office at Mammoth," he noted, looking around at the shop.

"A welcome one," I countered.

He stopped in front of one of the large framed photos. "Nice."

I didn't respond. It was the one of Dixie's delicious Dutch apple pie, and I swore that every time I looked at the photo, I could smell the warm cinnamon and sweet spiced apple from the day we'd done the photo session.

He glanced around the room at the other oversized photos. "Very professional." Continuing his walk, he headed toward a giant scone dripping in clotted cream. "Who's your photographer?"

"Local guy," I answered. I wasn't sure you could count former globe-trotting photojournalist Max Windsor as local, but he lived here now. I knew I was being unhelpful and borderline rude, but I truly just wanted him to go away.

I took a deep breath and another gulp of coffee and tried to adjust my attitude. "Are you staying in town?" I asked, striving for a polite tone.

"No, the producer booked me at a hotel in Des Moines." He continued his walk around the shop. I was going to have to stop him if he headed toward Dixie's kitchen. "Same one I stayed in the last time I was in Iowa."

I remembered that last time well, and I knew exactly which hotel because that was where he'd delivered his scathing remarks about the direction the magazine had been going under my leadership. In full hearing of my boss.

"Listen—" he began but stopped as the front door dinged and opened.

Sheriff Terry walked in.

Dino's eyes slid to mine, and his expression held a momentary flash of "You called the cops?"

I may have smirked a little, and though I wasn't proud of it, I enjoyed his off-balance reaction. Again, though our sheriff was a nice guy, in full law enforcement regalia, he could look pretty intimidating.

He stepped forward, towering over Dino. "I don't believe we've met." He held out his hand. "Sheriff Griffin."

Dino hesitated but reluctantly took the sheriff's hand. "Dino Dinelli."

"Is this where you warn me to watch myself because 'I'm in your town now' or something like that?" Dino laughed.

"Not unless you need to be warned about something." The sheriff didn't laugh. "Actually, I'm here to talk with Sugar." He tipped his head in my direction. I didn't know whether Dixie had shared my dislike for Dino with him or whether he was reading my body language, but in any case, I was happy for the rescue.

Don't you need to be going? Sheriff Terry didn't say it aloud, but it was certainly implied as he eyed Dino. From the look on Dino's face, he'd clearly gotten the message. Maybe it was a Jedi mind trick the sheriff had developed from years of dealing with people.

"I was on my way out." Dino headed for the door. "Nice place you've got here."

The bell dinged as he left, and I muttered, "Good riddance."

"I gather you don't much care for the guy." Sheriff Terry chuckled.

"You've got that right." I nodded. "Coffee?"

"Oh, man. Yes, please."

I headed to the kitchen area and grabbed another mug. I filled it and topped off my own as Dixie came in the back door.

"Your sheriff is out front."

"Not my—" She stopped midsentence as she spotted Sheriff Terry, who had appeared in the hallway.

"Here, let me grab one of those." He took a couple of the grocery bags she was carrying, and I grabbed another.

"Thanks," she responded.

We followed Dixie to the kitchen and slid the groceries onto the counter. The bell out front dinged again.

Busy morning.

"Be right there." I stuck my head out and saw that it was Tina Martin.

"Tina." I mouthed to Dixie and the sheriff.

"Listen," he said quietly, "I stopped by to let you know that Marla's house was broken into last night."

"Oh, no." Dixie made eye contact with me, and I knew she was thinking of my incident with the scarecrow, though she, to her credit, didn't bring it up.

"Here's the thing," the sheriff continued. "Mame seems to have developed a fondness for you two nuts, and I wondered if you wouldn't mind checking in on her later. She may need some support."

"Absolutely. Did she go to work?" I was free and could go right now.

"She did. The woman has perfect attendance, according to the people I talked to at the school when we were trying to verify her whereabouts the day of Marla's murder."

"And probably her method of coping as well," I added.

"Was anything taken?" Dixie asked.

"That's what we're trying to figure out, but without Marla to ask …" Sheriff Terry shrugged.

"How did they get in?" I wondered whether all the doors had been locked or not.

"Broke a window on the back side of the house." He shook his head. "That's part of what has Mame so upset. She didn't hear a thing."

"Helloo," Tina called out.

"Be right there," I answered.

"I'd appreciate you not sharing any details with …" the sheriff jabbed his thumb toward the front. "We want to see if this fits the MO of the other break-ins before the whole community gets wound up with word-of-mouth theories."

Dixie and I nodded.

"I'd better get out there before she comes looking for us." I picked up my coffee and paused. "Thanks for the rescue earlier."

"You bet."

Dixie gave us both a quizzical look and handed me a small plate of mini muffins she'd brought from home. I put it back down.

"No. I am not giving her one of those to nibble to death."

Dixie chuckled, then gave me the side-eye and put it back in my hand.

"Okay." I headed out front with the muffins and my coffee.

"Hi, Tina." Today, she was attired in a crimson dress with a wide brown suede belt and matching brown boots. The streak in her hair was gone. Who knew that kind of thing was so changeable?

"What's up?" I offered her the plate.

"You tell me." She picked up a mini muffin daintily. "I saw that Dino Diner guy come into your shop earlier."

I must have looked surprised.

"I was on my way to the Red Hen," she explained.

Tina wasn't a usual morning patron at the diner. She was more of a healthy smoothie type than an eggs and bacon type, so there must have been a reason for the exception.

"When I was walking back, I saw him opening the door to Sugar & Spice." She waited.

I didn't offer up any explanation.

"What did he want?" She was forced into direct interrogation by my lack of cooperation.

I caved. "Not sure. I think he was kind of looking around the square. Maybe getting a feel for the town." I shrugged. "You'd have to ask him."

"Hmmm." She looked over my shoulder. "Is Dixie here?" Tina must have heard some sound from the back. Probably the sheriff leaving through the back door.

"She's bringing in supplies."

Note to self: Not sure a security camera is needed when we have Tina.

Dixie appeared and greeted Tina.

"Dino Dinelli stopped by earlier," I filled in Dixie. "Tina was wondering why. Frankly, I was too."

"How did that go?" Dixie asked.

"Fine," I answered in what I thought was a very noncommittal tone.

Tina looked from Dixie to me and back again. Clearly, the woman had a nose for trouble and we hadn't been quite as neutral in our exchange as we'd thought.

"Is there a problem with the show?" Tina leaned on the counter. "Do you know when they are filming? I guess they may have to shut part of that section of the square down."

"No, no problems I'm aware of." I grabbed a cloth and

started wiping down the counter. "I hope that he behaves himself while he's in town is all. You know, he's not the kindest person in his reviews of restaurants."

"But what's not to love about the Red Hen?" Dixie asked.

"We love it." I raised an eyebrow. "I hope he does too."

"I heard they're going to pick people to be eating at the Red Hen while they're filming." Tina finished off her mini muffin.

Will wonders never cease?

It seemed Dixie had found the perfect serving size for a nibbler like Tina.

"Really?" Dixie raised her brows. "I thought since it's a reality show that it would be whoever was eating at the time."

"Apparently, it's not that real."

I wasn't that surprised. I knew the reality shows were at least lightly produced, some more than others. And when they involved big personalities like Dino's, they weren't going to be taking any chances.

"Toy could probably give you the lowdown on that." Dixie plucked the cloth from my hand and set it aside.

It seemed like Tina was focused on the *Dino's Diners* show and news of the break-in at Marla's hadn't reached her.

"She probably could, but she was not talking." Tina shrugged. "Something about a document they had her sign." Her watch buzzed, and she glanced at it. "Sorry, ladies. I'll see you later. I've got to get going."

"I bet they had her sign a document," I muttered as Tina took her leave.

"I feel so bad for Mame." Dixie headed toward the back. "That must be really unsettling, to have a break-in right next door."

"I imagine the lure of a house sitting empty was too tempting." Though I did know that the motion detector lights really lit up the front yard. "Sheriff Terry was right. If this is the same person, they know opportune locations and people's routines."

"Does it feel chilly in here to you?" she asked.

"It does, but I checked the thermostat and it's set at the usual," I responded.

"Must be the change in the weather." She shrugged. "I need to pull out my fall clothes."

Dixie and I finished up putting away the supplies.

Then she grabbed the folder I'd picked up from Lewis and sat down at the kitchen island to make notes.

I aimed myself toward my office, as I hadn't really had a chance to get started on anything before Dino had shown up.

It was quiet in the shop as we worked separately. I answered emails and did one final review of the proposal for the tearoom in a neighboring town. I needed to tackle the pie shop request next, but it was a little more complicated.

"Sugar, could you come here a minute?" Dixie called from what sounded like the storeroom.

I followed her voice, but she wasn't in the storeroom. She was standing in the doorway of our bathroom.

Oh, no. Plumbing repairs were not in our budget.

The on-premises bathroom was small, and certain things were required by code, but it was a very utilitarian bathroom. Only the basics. It had to have been the stool or the sink. Nothing else was there. I hoped that whatever it was, it hadn't been leaking for a long time.

As I stepped beside her, I didn't see any water on the floor. She pointed upward.

The small window on the outside wall was open. It was a rectangular-shaped opening, and we'd hung some simple curtains over it. Most of the time, we actually forgot it was there. But right now, the curtains fluttered in the breeze.

"I guess that's why it seems so chilly in here." I hugged my sweater around me. "Think we ought to let the sheriff know?"

"I suppose we should." She stepped back. "I'd like to close it, but I don't want to touch it in case they need to do fingerprints."

"I'll call him and see what he wants us to do." Walking to my office for my phone, I picked it up and dialed Sheriff Terry's number.

"He wasn't that far away and said he'd head back here," I reported to Dixie, who hadn't moved from her spot.

The sheriff took one look at our open window, tore off a paper towel, then reached up and closed it. "I guess the good news is they didn't need to break anything to get in."

"Not sure if that's good news or bad news." Dixie shook her head.

"I'll have the crime lab people dust it." The sheriff backed out of the small room. "But I'll bet it's like the others. No fingerprints."

"Sugar has checked her office and doesn't think anything is missing." Dixie frowned. "No cash missing anyway."

"Where do you keep the cash you have?" he asked.

"In this box." I held up a pink-striped cupcake box.

"You're not serious." He raised a brow.

"Unfortunately, I am." I opened the box so he could see. There was under twenty dollars in the box. Mostly ones, a couple of fives, and some change. "It could be the location worked in our favor. Maybe the thief didn't think to look in here."

"Have you walked the whole place?" Sheriff Terry moved

down the hallway and into the front of the shop. "Like out here?"

"Not yet," Dixie answered, following him.

"Anything else of value that could have been taken?" He walked around the room as if seeing it for the first time.

"Not really." I walked the room too. Dixie paced. "I can't come up with anything."

"Sugar, Terry, come here." Dixie had stopped at the front counter. "Look."

We joined her.

The large glass jar for skate park contributions was sitting on the edge of the counter. A jar that had been empty now contained a hundred-dollar bill.

What the heck? I hadn't noticed it before. Though the paper that gave details on the fundraiser covered part of the jar. Had the Cash Burglar brought cash? Had someone snuck in and slipped a C-note in the jar?

"Who else has been in here this morning?" The sheriff carefully turned the jar.

"You, Dino, and Tina," I answered. "If someone had come in while we were in the back, the bell would've dinged."

"Okay." The sheriff picked up the jar. "Sorry, but I'm going to need to take this with me."

"You're closed for the rest of the day." His serious tone left no room for discussion.

Unlike for most of the places around the square, that wasn't going to be a huge inconvenience for us. We weren't dependent on our storefront.

"I'll try to get techs here as soon as possible. In the meantime, go home, go to lunch, whatever."

Dixie and I looked at each other. "Red Hen?"

~

"Cluck." The chicken chime over the door announced us as we entered, and the kitschy décor never failed to delight me. Rooster tiles, chicken statues, and baby chick salt and pepper shakers lined the walls. And Toy George in her "Head Chick" apron had already spotted us.

"Heard you had a break-in." She ushered us to a booth in the back, where it was a little quieter.

"How does that happen?" I whispered to Dixie as we slid into the booth.

"Terry called in his location while he was at our shop. Somebody's son or daughter or spouse or cousin works at the Jameson County Sheriff's Office, and whoosh"—she waved an arm—"the St. Ignatius communications network is off and running."

My iced tea appeared on the table; the "Head Chick" knew I usually switched from coffee at this time of day. "Dixie, what'll you have?"

"Lemonade, please."

"Be back in two shakes of a lamb's tail."

I didn't know exactly how fast a lamb shook its tail, but Toy was back at the table with Dixie's drink in no time.

She slid in beside me. "So what happened? Was it the Cash Burglar?" She fanned her face with one of the menus. I wasn't sure why she even brought us menus. I knew the offerings by heart, and other than the specials, the menu never changed. One of the things I loved about the place.

"We don't know." Dixie shrugged. "Nothing taken. Not even any cash."

I let Dixie take the lead. Though most of the locals and the Ren Hen regulars in particular had taken me under their wing, I still fell into the category of "not from here." I knew it took several generations of procreation before you lost that distinction. Apparently, Dixie wasn't going to share about the large bill that had appeared in the skate park donation jar.

"Not even cash, huh? That's strange." Toy stood and pulled out her order pad. No high-tech order pads at this diner. "Specials are pot roast and a meatloaf sandwich. What are you having today?"

"I'll take the meatloaf sandwich." No hesitation on my part. I'd tried it before, and it had never disappointed.

"I'll do the same." Dixie nodded.

Toy jotted down our order, tore off a ticket, and handed it to a waitress who was passing by. "Take that to the kitchen, hon."

The girl nodded and kept moving. Toy scurried back up to the front of the diner to take care of the small line of people waiting to pay.

"Must be shorthanded again." I smiled.

"Seems to be the way of things, doesn't it?" Dixie turned in her seat and eyed the full restaurant. "I don't understand these break-ins. It sounds like, from what Terry shared, that there's very little money involved. What would be the motive?"

I hadn't a clue.

In a very short time, our meals arrived, and as we dug in, we talked about the projects we had in play, the timing of the next photo shoot, and whether we needed to invest in a camera at the front and back doors. I jotted notes on a "Red Hen Diner" napkin.

By the time we were finished, we had a rough idea of the timeline for the projects and how they intersected. And a vague idea of what type of security camera we were interested in.

We could relocate to my dining room table for the rest of the day.

Dixie would ask Hirsh to give us some ideas on ease of installation. And I would call Max to coordinate with him on scheduling photo shoots.

As we walked back to the shop to see whether we could pick up the two folders of recipes, I called Mame's number and left her a message asking her to let me know when she would be home.

As off-kilter as we were feeling after finding a window open, I couldn't even imagine how worried she was feeling after a break-in right next door.

12

e settled in at the big table in my dining room and spread out the recipes. Mame called and let me know that she'd be home by three o'clock.

She called back to say it might be three-thirty. Then she called back again and said, no, it would probably be more like three-fifteen. Of course, a break-in next door would rattle anyone. Though probably, if the break-in had been at my neighbor's house, Mrs. Pickett would have been sure I was somehow responsible.

Dixie and I looked through the bread recipes and began the sorting process. Each section of the book got its own pile: Traditional Breads, Sweet Breads, Rolls and Muffins, and Family Favorites. The latter was for recipes that had been passed down from generation to generation. We were in good shape with the first three categories but didn't have enough in the Family Favorites pile.

Many of the current residents came from families that had founded St. Ignatius, so hopefully, I would be able to round up enough to fill in. I made a note to discuss it with Lewis at our next meeting.

It did look like the half recipe that Lewis had provided me matched with a second part among the papers Mame had given me. Dixie was going to take a closer look at it and see whether it was one that we wanted to include. If so, I'd have to fess up to Lewis that I had some notes from Mame.

By the time three o'clock rolled around, we had gotten a great start and it felt like the book was coming together. Dixie packed up to leave. She would stop by her brother's place and pick up some info he had about security cameras. I put the recipes and the sticky notes with questions we'd attached to them into separate folders. Then I grabbed my keys and headed toward Mame's house.

I pulled into the driveway. In broad daylight, all the fall decorations on the front porch of the main house looked festive. In my defense, it had been dark when I was there the last time and I'd been intent on navigating the bushes and the drive and making my way back to Mame and the carriage house.

Parking my car, I got out and looked around. It truly was a gorgeous Victorian-style house, and the exterior of the carriage house was the same style. But because the carriage house hadn't been built as a living space, the interior was much more modern. My guess from what I'd seen was that the remodel had happened sometime in the seventies.

I knocked on the door, and it didn't take Mame long to open it. She was still in her work clothes and invited me in to wait while she changed.

"Have you been over to the house?" I asked.

"I have." She nodded. "Well, with the deputies but not since."

"It's hard to know if anything is missing when it's not your house. But you've been in Marla's home frequently, so if anyone might know, it would be you."

She headed down the small hallway to change her clothes and was back in a jiffy.

"Maybe if we went over there together, it would be easier," I offered.

"Oh, would you?" Her face showed relief. "That would be great."

Mame picked up her keys from a dish on the hall table, and we walked across the park-like back lawn. She inserted the key, took a deep breath, and slowly opened the door.

"I guess we could've gone in the front," she said, "but I've always used the back door since I moved here, so I go this way out of habit."

Going in the back, we stepped into an enclosed sunroom with a vaulted ceiling.

"So pretty." I admired the bright, flowered area rug and the twin wicker rocking chairs. There was a wicker table positioned between them.

"We sat out here with a couple of lemonades or tea a lot," Mame said quietly. "And talked."

I touched her arm. I'd never had the experience of losing someone I cared about suddenly and then needing to go through their things. I guess it might have seemed sudden to some when my father passed away, but he'd been killing himself with alcohol for years. And at the time, I hadn't seen him in months.

This situation was way different. Marla had been there for Mame day after day; they'd shared what had happened during their days, and then Marla had been gone.

She opened the door from the sunroom into the main

house. It led to the large kitchen. It had obviously been updated over the years, but the remodels had been done with an eye to the feel of the house. Tall cream-colored cupboards reached toward a coffered ceiling, and the stone countertops were a soft beige.

The silence was kind of eerie, and I could see why Mame had been reluctant to come by herself. Our steps on the hard-wood floors echoed as we walked toward the front of the house. I flipped on lights as we went, even though it was still daylight out.

"Where was the window that was broken?" I asked.

"The back of the house." Mame pointed.

As we moved into the living room, or what would have been called the parlor, nothing seemed out of place. There was a built-in bookcase on one side and a fireplace on the other, as well as several lovely antique pieces and a mahogany library table with framed photos lined up on top of it.

I picked up one of the photos from the table. "Is this you?" It was a happy shot of three women with their arms around each other. I recognized younger versions of Mame and Marla. A laughing blonde woman was standing between them.

Mame moved beside me to look. "Yes, that's me with Marla and our friend DeeDee." She turned away.

Giving her some space, I moved to the next room. The dining room had not been updated, but I imagined Marla hadn't spent much time in there. It was a lot of house for one person, so she'd probably focused on the areas she'd used most. Still, the dining room was impressive, with a large walnut dining table. And the sideboard looked to be Eastlake like the table I'd spotted at Mame's. It had a marble serving area and was in great shape. What on earth was

Mame going to do with this much stuff and this much space?

"Do you notice anything that's missing or off?" I asked.

Mame walked slowly through the room. "It's hard to say," she said, glancing around the room with a frown. She reached for one of the dishes on the sideboard, knocking it off its stand with a clatter. "Oops."

I winced. Mame was a bumbler. Some would say "a bull in a china shop" or, as my Aunt Cricket often referred to our cousin Paula, "a tornado in a trailer park." Whatever name you gave it, the poor woman's coordination was somehow always a bit off, which resulted in butterfingered knock-overs, surprise stumbles, and inadvertent spills.

"Let's check the living room," I suggested. We made our way back to the parlor.

Mame's eyes scanned the shelves, the mantel, and the curio. She shook her head. "Nothing missing as far as I can tell."

We moved upstairs to the bedrooms, checking drawers and closets. It looked like the drawers were in disarray, and that didn't seem like Marla. But who knew, right? If she'd been going through something in the days before her death, she may have been a little scattered.

"I don't think I've ever been in these rooms," Mame said softly. "At least not since we were teenagers and spent the night at each other's homes."

"Was this her room then?" I asked.

"No, hers was the smaller one down the hall." Mame pointed. "This bigger bedroom belonged to her parents back then."

We moved from room to room, with Mame getting quieter and quieter.

"I can't be of any help up here." Her shoulders drooped.

"Okay. Let's head back downstairs." This was turning out to be way harder than I'd expected and extremely emotional for Mame.

As we made our way down the beautiful staircase, I trailed my fingers on the tiger walnut wood and imagined sweeping down it in a fancy dress. But that would probably be when my own inner china shop bull showed up, and I'd tumble down the stairs.

"It's a fantastic house, Mame." I completed the flight of stairs without mishap. "I know you probably haven't had time to even think about what you want to do with it."

"It's just a house." Her whole body sagged. "But it does hold a lot of memories. I'm sad that there's nobody left from Marla's family to remember them."

"That is sad." I paused for a moment, thinking about where all the items would go. The people who would perhaps buy them, appreciate them. But they wouldn't know the history. They wouldn't have the memories each item represented.

"Thank you," Mame said quietly. "For being here, for understanding."

"When you get ready to decide what to do with everything, let me know, and I'll be back." I put my arm around her. "It's a lot to deal with, and I know it doesn't feel like it right now, but it's really an honor that Marla trusted you to be the one to sort things out."

She nodded, her eyes filling with tears, but a small smile broke through as she raised her head and straightened her shoulders.

"All right, where haven't we been?" I needed to help her stay on task so she could report back to Sheriff Terry.

"Marla's office." She pointed to a hallway. "She turned the downstairs study into her office."

We moved toward the office and opened the door to what would have seemed to most a very tidy study, but I was learning that Marla had been a whole other level of neatnik.

There were no papers strewn across the floor, books pulled haphazardly from the shelves, or desk drawers standing open. However, there was a lack of order that even I could see.

"Someone has been in here," Mame whispered. "Marla had an 'a place for everything and everything in its place' attitude. Things have been moved around."

"Whoever was here was definitely looking for something." I leaned over the desk, noting papers that looked like they'd been leafed through.

"I don't know what they were looking for, but there's one thing I hope they didn't find." Mame moved to the bookshelves and reached up for a large book. Pulling it down, she opened it to reveal it was more of a box than a book.

Inside were stacks of neatly bound journals. "Marla's journals." She touched the covers. "She always wrote something about her day. Kept a diary when we were kids."

"At least those are safe." I let out a breath I hadn't realized I was holding, glad that something so personal hadn't been messed with.

"What did Marla use her office for?" I asked, realizing that when I'd met with Marla, she hadn't said anything about what she did apart from volunteering at the historical society.

"She mostly used it for stuff for her volunteer work." Mame straightened some papers on the desk. "And since she retired, for research she was doing on her family. I think realizing that no one would come after her, she got interested in those who had gone before."

Sure made sense to me. With business picking up at Sugar & Spice, I had been too busy to spend much time on my own genealogy work.

"What did she do before she retired?" I looked at the books on the shelves that took up one wall. There were a lot of local history books.

"She worked at the courthouse," Mame explained. "She started right out of high school but worked her way up."

"What an interesting woman," I said, stepping closer to look at a volume of Walt Whitman poems. "I wish I would have had the opportunity to know her better."

"You would have liked her." Mame smiled, a glimmer of pride in her eyes. "I think you're like her in a lot of ways. You're determined. You care about people."

"Thank you, Mame," I said, touched that she thought so. "That means a lot."

We finished in the office and closed the door behind us. Nothing was missing as far as Mame could tell.

"Any place you can think of where Marla might have kept cash?" I asked. If this had been the Cash Burglar, it looked like they'd struck out.

"She kept some cash in her purse, but I have her purse at my place," Mame answered. "The sheriff gave it to me, but I haven't been able to bring myself to look through it. It seems wrong to go through someone else's purse."

I got it. I'd probably feel that way too.

"Wait a minute." Mame stopped in her tracks. "Marla always kept money in the sugar bowl in the kitchen. I didn't check it."

Heading to the kitchen, we looked around and then began opening cupboards, looking for the sugar bowl.

"What does it look like?" I asked, opening the cupboard by the sink.

"Like this." Mame turned toward me holding a lovely porcelain sugar bowl painted with pastel flowers.

I silently prayed she wouldn't drop it.

My prayers were answered as she carefully placed it on the counter and lifted the lid. We peered inside.

Nothing.

"How much money did Marla usually keep in it?"

"Not a lot." Mame put the lid back on. "Enough that if a kid came to the door, like a Girl Scout selling cookies or a Little Leaguer selling chocolate bars, she could buy something from them. She loved those chocolate bars."

The flicker of a smile washed over Mame's ruddy face.

I closed the cupboard I had opened, and as I did, I noticed a wooden box that seemed out of place in the kitchen on the counter. It looked familiar.

"What's this?" I asked, pointing at the box.

Mame was still touching the sugar bowl, lost in thought.

I could have sworn it was a duplicate of the box I'd seen at Lewis Brimley's office. Same size, same walnut color, same brass.

"Oh, that." She looked up. "Lewis Brimley brought it over yesterday. He said Marla had had it at the historical society office. Lewis said she'd had some old recipes and notes in it. He acted like it was in their way at the historical society, so he brought it to me. I brought it over here. It used to belong to our friend DeeDee. But anyway, at some point, she gave it to Marla."

"It's a cool box." I ran my fingers over the wood. The top

had a hand carving of the profile of a woman with long, flowing hair. I opened it. Empty.

"People collect these kinds of folk art items." I had seen a trunk done in a similar fashion at Auntie's Antiques a while back and been amazed at the price. I hadn't known that type of thing was so collectible. The trunk was much larger and probably what they used to refer to as a hope chest. But if I remembered correctly, it was marked at a couple of thousand dollars.

"I guess it should go to DeeDee's family, but I wouldn't even know how to start to find any relatives."

"What about her husband?" I was sure Dixie and Greer had both talked about him like he still lived in the community.

"Oh, him." Mame blew out a breath. "I'm kind of scared of him."

"Why?" I turned to look at her.

"He was never very nice to us. To DeeDee's friends. And after DeeDee left town, he blamed Marla."

"How could Marla have been to blame?'

"I don't know for sure, but Marla found out that whenever DeeDee met with the guy she eventually ran off with, she told Dwayne she'd been with Marla."

"That's crazy." I was defensive on Marla's behalf. "She didn't know, did she?"

"No." Mame shook her head vigorously. "She wouldn't have been a part of that."

"But you and Marla were such good friends with DeeDee that you must have known about it, right?"

"Kind of yes and kind of no." Mame stood thinking. "I mean, we knew something was up, but DeeDee had kind of done her own thing since she got married. She started selling real estate, and we thought she must have been busy with that and her new life. And didn't have time for us anymore. But it turned out she was busy in a different way."

"Wow, it must have been hard when she left town, then."

"It was." Mame paused. "I wish I could let her know about Marla."

We stood in silence for a few minutes.

Me thinking about what a tough job Mame had ahead of her and, I'm sure, Mame thinking about her two friends.

I reached over and touched her arm.

"Well, we'll deal with the box later." I closed it and pushed it to the back of the counter. That was one heavy box. "Maybe later you can offer it to DeeDee's husband—" I stopped. "What's his name?"

"Dwayne."

Whoa. That's a lot of Ds. Dwayne and DeeDee Darling. It sounds like a match made in heaven.

But apparently, it wasn't.

13

*A*s I walked away from the carriage house after making sure Mame was okay and set for the evening, I could feel fall in the air. A wind gust blew a few colorful leaves from the tall oak in the front, and they drifted down playfully. The emotion of the afternoon's tasks still weighed heavily on me, but I took a deep breath and climbed into the Jeep.

As I was about to back out and turn toward my house, my phone buzzed. I pulled it out of my bag and saw Greer's name on the screen.

"Hey, Greer," I answered, a smile already forming.

"Sugar, dear ..." Greer's voice was warm and friendly. A balm to my chaotic thoughts. "I wondered if you could stop by for a moment. There's something I'd like to show you."

"Of course," I replied without hesitation. "I'm actually nearby." Maybe I could get her opinion on families I might tap for the Family Favorites section of the historical society cookbook while I was there. Greer knew everyone in town.

The drive to the Good Life retirement community was

short, and as I approached Greer's place, I could see her sitting on her small front patio, bundled up in a rust fleece jacket, amidst her red and orange fall décor. It looked like the display might have grown since I had last been there. Frenchie was wearing a matching doggie coat and cuddled next to Greer.

She stood when she saw me, tucking Frenchie under her arm. "Come in, come in," she urged, opening the door wide.

"Would you like some tea?"

"I would love some," I declared, looking forward to the hot spiced tea Greer favored.

Greer disappeared into the kitchen for a moment and returned with a steaming pot of tea and two cute pumpkin teacups. She poured the tea and handed me a cup before settling into her chair across from where I'd parked myself on the sofa. She had discarded her jacket and bent down to help Frenchie out of hers.

"What's on your mind?" I asked, taking in the luscious smell of the cinnamon before tasting the tea.

"I was thinking about that project you're working on for the historical society, and I was sure we'd tried to do something like that way back when I used to volunteer there."

"I heard something about that from Marla when I first met with her." I took a slow sip.

"I did some asking around, and Bunny Hopper was on the board at the same time as me."

Every time I heard Bunny's name, I was suddenly back in junior high and I couldn't hold back a snicker. It didn't help that the tiny white-haired lady fit the moniker to the nth degree. I took a sip of my tea and tried to maintain my composure.

"That little pack rat keeps everything," Greer continued.

"And I thought she might have some notes or something to help you. I'm sure the current board wouldn't think to ask us elders." She made a face.

Curiosity piqued, I leaned forward. "And?"

"And leave it to Bunny." She reached beside her chair and pulled out a pack of yellowed recipe file cards tied together with a red satin ribbon. "She came up with these. I thought you might like to take a look."

I took the packet from her, the ribbon nearly disintegrating in my hands as I untied it. "Wow, thank you."

"Don't thank me. Thank Bunny." Greer laughed. "I probably had a similar packet but threw it out years ago. Or it's in a box in the attic."

She meant the attic at my house. Her house. The house where I currently lived. I'd been in that attic retrieving items for Greer zillions of times. I wasn't sure we would have been able to locate a small group of cards like this. Or at least not this year, anyway.

"This is fantastic." I carefully thumbed through the recipe cards. "We're short on what Marla put together before ... you know."

"How is the investigation going?" she asked, reaching for the teapot to refill our cups. "I hear there have been some burglaries around town and they think her murder might be linked to a break-in."

It seemed that news of the break-ins had traveled like wildfire. There was no keeping those details contained any longer.

I filled Greer in on the broken window at the shop, the mysterious large bill that had shown up, and the break-in at Marla's house.

"That's where I was when you called." I took another sip of tea. "I was helping Mame go through the house to see if she could identify things that might be missing."

"And were there things missing?" Greer leaned forward.

"It seems like it was only a small amount of cash she'd kept on hand. Like the other break-ins."

"The Cash Burglar strikes again." She sat back in her chair.

The catchy name has also clearly spread like wildfire.

Greer said that Bunny had told her I could keep the recipe cards as long as I needed them, so I tucked them in my bag. After a cozy chat about the book she was reading and the upcoming Harvest Festival, I helped carry the teapot and cups to her kitchen.

"You didn't mention the visit from Dino Diner," Greer noted as we were rinsing out the dishes. "I gathered that you don't like the guy."

"I'm just afraid he's going to be cruel to Toy and derogatory about the Red Hen." I dried the last dish, setting it aside. "And then I'll have to punch him."

Greer laughed. "That would make for some good TV." She opened a cupboard and set the cups inside.

"That's the problem." I moved to the living room and started gathering my things. "That's all he is about. Ratings. Not people."

Greer patted my arm. "It's nice of you to worry about Toy George, but she's a tough cookie. I think she'll be fine."

After giving Frenchie some belly rubs and hugging Greer goodbye, I headed home. Or the house that I considered home. I hadn't really thought much about it until now, but it must have been difficult for Greer to leave a house that held memories. Like Marla's house had held memories for her.

Greer had one son, who lived in Minneapolis and didn't visit his mother as often as I thought he should.

I pulled into the driveway and sat looking at the well-kept little white Queen Anne. I loved the gingerbread trim on the front and the maple in the yard, which was in the process of turning a bright crimson. Maybe I'd get some fall decorations for myself. I knew the hardware store had a ton of choices. I wasn't ready to go all out like Marla, but something cheerful on the porch would look nice. Maybe colorful mums or a pumpkin or two.

I grabbed my bag, pushed the car door closed, and trekked toward the front door.

Catching movement out of the corner of my eye, I started.

I'd been so absorbed in thinking about decorating my porch, I hadn't seen Mrs. Pickett standing at the edge of her yard, leaning on a rake, arms crossed, and brow furrowed.

"Afternoon, Sugar," she greeted me, though her tone was far from friendly. "Your big blow-up jack-o'-lantern and fake hay bales have blown in my yard."

Those weren't mine. But as I opened my mouth to tell her that, she flipped around, set her rake aside, and returned to her house, slamming the door as she went inside.

With a sigh, I set my things inside my house and went to retrieve the very large inflatable jack-o'-lantern that was leering at me from under Mrs. Pickett's big oak tree. He was taller than me by at least a foot. And the wind had picked up, pushing the inflatable in my face.

"You're coming with me, Jack," I told him, grabbing the puffy pumpkin by his orange cheek. As I did, he let out a creepy *Ooooo* sound.

"Now, none of that." I dragged him along. Certain from the direction of the wind that he'd come from the house on the *other* side of Mrs. Pickett's, I'd check with them first. Maybe they were missing a jack-o'-lantern guy.

I knocked on the door, and a young woman and two school-aged children came to it. "I think your pumpkin may have blown next door." I pointed at the inflatable I had in my grip. My friend, Jack, continued to *Ooooo* and grin. And was beginning to bounce against my side as the wind increased.

"Oh, gosh. So sorry about that." The woman looked relieved, and I guessed it might have been because it was me at her door and not Mrs. Pickett.

"No worries. He actually got caught under Mrs. Pickett's tree; otherwise, with this wind, he might have continued down the street, visiting other neighbors." I grinned at the kids.

"Thanks for bringing it back." The woman smiled. "Maybe we'll put him in the garage until we can get some rope and tie him down."

"Let me help you get him in there," I offered. "We don't want him to take off while you're getting the door open."

I helped her get the big jack-o'-lantern in the garage, and then we gathered up the fake hay bales and stowed them too. Then I finally made my way back home.

"Now, that's how neighbors are supposed to act," I muttered under my breath as I passed Mrs. Pickett's house.

As soon as I entered my house, Ernest greeted me with an irritated meow.

"All right, I hear you." I headed to the kitchen to get fresh water and food.

Just call me cat staff.

The pay wasn't much, but the benefits made up for it.

My stomach growled, reminding me that it had been a long while since lunch, and I turned my attention to what I had on hand to feed myself. When I opened the refrigerator, the offerings did not look promising at all. A half-empty carton of eggs, a container of milk, and a package of cheese. I pulled open the crisper to see a few veggies and decided there were enough to pull together an omelet.

I chopped up the vegetables—some green onions and a bell pepper—and whisked the eggs with a splash of milk. Adding the cheese, I poured it all into a pan. Stepping past Ernest, I opened the pantry. Hopefully, I had some bread, because with toast, I thought I could call this a meal.

As I buttered the toast, I began to review the day's events. The visit from Dino, the open window at the shop, reviewing the recipes with Dixie, going through Marla's house with Mame, and my talk with Greer. And I couldn't forget my windy battle with Mr. Jack-O'-Lantern.

What a day. The cheesy omelet was both tasty and comforting.

As I finished and then carried my dishes to the counter, it hit me. The box at Marla's house—it looked so familiar. But it wasn't just that I'd seen it at Lewis's office. It had also been on the counter at the historical society on the first day I met with Marla. I hadn't noticed the carving on top because it had been open.

But thinking back, I hadn't seen it on the day she died. Or didn't remember it, anyway. It must have been there. Not in the same spot, though, if Lewis had said it was in the way.

I hoped Mame could bring herself to take it to Dwayne Darling. Something like that needed to stay in the family.

I rinsed the dishes and set them aside to dry. Ernest rubbed against my ankle, prodding me to give him some attention.

Glancing over at the clock, I was surprised by how late it

was. Tomorrow, I'd give Mame a call and see whether I couldn't nudge her about the box. Maybe with a little encouragement, she'd be more comfortable about returning it to Dwayne. It might well have been a part of his family's legacy.

If Dwayne didn't want it, the historical society would surely be interested in a piece that represented local history.

14

The next morning, before I left the house, I made myself a note to call Mame later in the day and talk to her about the antique wooden box. I knew that even though I was up early, she would have been up earlier and at the school already, so there was no point in calling her now.

Parking my Jeep next to Dixie's pickup at the back of the shop, I reached in for my things. It was warmer today, with a bit of lingering summer. I'd donned tan khakis and a deep-turquoise turtleneck, but I'd grabbed a jacket just in case.

As soon as I stepped inside, I could tell Dixie had already been busy. The aroma of coffee mixed in the air with that of baking … scones? Cranberry orange, lemon blueberry, brown sugar cardamon? I couldn't remember what kind, and frankly, I didn't care. I loved them all.

"Come with me." Dixie handed me a mug filled with steaming coffee and crooked her finger, heading to the front of the shop. She had some printed info on different types of security cameras fanned out on the counter.

I looked through the papers and filled her in on my time at

128

Marla's house, how emotional it had been for Mame, and the missing cash.

"Nothing else missing?" She settled on a stool, crossing her long, jean-clad legs. Like me, she'd gone for a lighter-weight top today. A long-sleeved forest-green tee that set off her gorgeous red locks.

"Not as far as Mame could tell," I answered.

"That's odd." She tapped her chin while she thought out loud. "An empty house, lots of items of value, and only that little bit of cash taken."

"But that does match with the Cash Burglar's other break-ins," I noted, enjoying my coffee. "How long before the scones are ready?" I inclined my head toward the kitchen.

"Not long." She grinned. "I've set a timer."

"Oh, and also this." I pulled the recipe cards from my pocket and explained the call from Greer. And the loan of the cards from Bunny Hopper.

"That's awesome." Dixie reached for the cards right as the buzzer went off in the kitchen.

I started to get up, but she waved me off. "You stay put and look at the security camera info. Hirsh and I narrowed it down to three choices, but I'd like to talk about what we really need."

Reaching into one of the drawers, I found a pen and made a few notes in the margins of the printouts as I read through the details.

In a short time, Dixie was back with more coffee and two scones. Cranberry orange. My favorite.

"Let them cool." She waved my hand away.

"At first pass, I'd say the more basic the better for the camera." I tapped my pen on one of the papers. "It's not like we're in the big city and dealing with a smash-and-grab crime spree."

I broke off a piece of one of the scones and popped it into my mouth. "They're cool enough." I grinned.

Dixie laughed. "To hear the talk around town, we might as well be dealing with a major crime spree." She tasted one of the scones herself and closed her eyes. I could tell she was analyzing flavor blends.

I took another bite of my scone and closed my eyes too, but I wasn't analyzing anything. I was enjoying the pure pleasure of the flaky treat. "These scones are delicious." I was trying to pace myself, but they were so perfect with coffee. "Your Aunt Bertie's recipe?"

Dixie nodded.

"It does seem like folks are up in arms about the burglaries. Even though the losses are minimal." She frowned.

The reactions had surprised me a little, but after finding the open window yesterday, I kind of got it. It was an invasion. In a community like St. Ignatius, where some people didn't even lock their doors during the day and left their keys in their cars—and if you lost your wallet, there was no question it would be returned to you intact. The burglaries were a loss of trust.

We moved on to discussing the recipes, and Dixie was excited to try a couple she'd not made before. She set aside two of the cards and started a list of ingredients she would need.

The shop's doorbell chimed, and I have to admit, my first thought was to hope it wasn't Tina this morning. Thankfully, Sheriff Terry walked in.

"Morning, Dixie, Sugar." He nodded, joining us at the counter.

Dixie rose and headed toward the kitchen. She came back with a mug for the sheriff, a glass of milk for herself, and a plate with some warm scones. Her cheeks were flushed from the oven. Or at least it might have been from the oven, but it could have been from her proximity to Sheriff Terry.

"I'm sure you noticed we finished up with your bathroom yesterday." He accepted the coffee. "No prints. Nothing. In fact, it doesn't even look like anyone came in through the window."

"Well, that is a relief in a way, I guess." Dixie brushed her hair back. "Though it still leaves us with some unanswered questions. Did they get interrupted? Change their mind?"

"Hard to say." Sheriff Terry shook his head.

"Did Mame call you about the break-in at Marla's house?" I asked.

"She did." His brow furrowed. "Like the rest. Only cash, nothing else. It's the same pattern all over town. Expensive items are left behind—jewelry, electronics, credit cards— things that are easy to carry and easy to convert to cash."

"That's puzzling." Dixie slid onto the stool beside me.

"In total, there's probably only been a few hundred dollars. But it really has people psyched up." He rubbed his forehead with one hand and grabbed a scone with the other.

"Especially with an unsolved murder," I added.

"And there's that." He nodded. Leaning a hip on the counter, he picked up one of the pages I'd written notes on. "What's this?"

"We've been thinking about installing a security camera." Dixie nodded toward the front door. "Not like one that's monitored by a security company or anything but a simple one. Maybe it will help scare off our town thief."

The sheriff nodded thoughtfully. "Not a bad idea." He

picked up another of the papers and looked at it. "You know you may want to do front and back."

We'd been talking about only one in the front, but I could see his point. His phone buzzed, and he looked at it, picked up another scone, and headed for the door with a wave.

We both looked up as the bell dinged again. This time, it *was* Tina Martin, and she appeared to be a bit frazzled. I knew frazzled, as I was often not quite together first thing in the morning. But that wasn't Tina's usual.

"Good morning, ladies." Today's outfit was over-the-top, full-on fall. with rust-colored suede thigh-high boots, a tunic-length camel jacket over a bright-red V-neck sweater, and a long, plaid scarf dramatically flung around her neck.

"Why do I suddenly feel underdressed?" I muttered. Tina didn't hear me, but Dixie did and nearly snorted her milk.

Tina set her matching plaid purse on the counter. "Have you heard about the big commotion at the Red Hen this morning?"

"No. What happened?" I leaned forward, elbows on the counter, chin in my hands. Dixie frowned at me.

"It was awful." Tina rubbed her temples with her fingers as if to ward off a pending headache.

Yep, you guessed it. Those fingers were tipped with bright-red polish that perfectly matched her sweater. "The film crew for that reality show, *Dino's Diner*," she continued, "were there trying to shoot a promo."

"Seems like a good thing," I said, egging her on. "Then what happened?"

"Well, they asked some of the regulars to move from their usual seats. You know, for better angles. Of course, the regulars weren't having any of it. They flat out refused to move." She let out a huff.

Dixie raised a brow and looked at me.

Ah, that explained the runway-ready look Tina was sporting. She'd been at the Red Hen, hoping to be in the promo video. I wondered what she'd ordered. I wasn't sure that Toy George had healthy smoothies on the menu. The Healthy Options section she'd recently added had turkey bacon instead of regular pork bacon and egg whites for those watching their cholesterol.

"I can see how that would ruffle some feathers." Dixie pushed the plate of scones toward Tina, and I glared at her. "The usuals at the Red Hen can be set in their ways and territorial about their spots for sure."

"Exactly." Tina hadn't noticed the plate of scones, and I reached out and pushed it back toward Dixie. "It turned into quite a scene. The producer was trying to reason with them, but you know how people can be."

"It's almost a second home to some folks," I agreed, thinking of the people who'd been there every time I'd been at the diner. The Red Hen Diner was a staple in town, more important than the courthouse. And the town was fiercely loyal to its routines.

"Old Wally yelled at the producer." Tina paused for effect.

No big explanation needed there. Everyone knew that Old Wally Nelson always yelled. He was hard of hearing and didn't ever realize how loud his voice was. Everybody was used to it, and most didn't think anything of it. He couldn't help it.

"The producer got all up in Old Wally's face and told him to sit down and be quiet. And then Young Wally jumped up to defend him. So did Toy. Everyone was yelling at once. Then Jeri Beetles threw a pie, and it hit the producer upside the head. You know she's got quite an arm. She was all-state in girls' softball."

"What kind of pie?" I couldn't look at Dixie.

She cleared her throat, and I knew she was having trouble holding on as well. "And then what happened, Tina?"

"It was awful," Tina continued, unfazed. "Nate Berg, from the paper, started taking pictures with his phone, and then everyone had their phones out snapping photos. Somebody—I think it was Leela Harper—called the sheriff."

So that was the call the sheriff took while he was here. Quite the picture.

"Wow," I got out, not quite suppressing a grin even though I tried.

"Sorry we missed that." Dixie finally looked at me, her hand over her mouth, trying to maintain her composure.

I looked away.

"I'd better get going." Tina collected her purse from the counter, not noticing our efforts to hold on and still not noticing the scones. She headed purposefully toward the door.

Ah, my scones are safe.

Dixie and I waited until she was gone and the door closed completely. Then all bets were off.

"Ha!" I let out the breath I'd been holding. "I would've paid for a front-row seat to that."

"'What kind of pie?'" Dixie snorted. "Seriously, that was your question?"

"I wanted to make sure I had the full picture." I held up my hands like I was framing a shot.

"Can't you just see Old Wally yelling at that Hollywood producer?" Dixie hooted. "Poor Wally. He doesn't even know he's being loud."

"I can, and ..." A giggle broke through at the thought. "And

Jeri Beetles with her killer arm. And apparently very good aim."

"Assault with a deadly pie," Dixie deadpanned—which set us off again.

We'd finally stopped giggling and I was mopping my eyes with a paper towel when a new visitor arrived.

"Hey, everyone," Disco greeted us like we were part of an adoring crowd. "Did you hear about the huge hullabaloo at the Red Hen this morning?"

"Tina was here and told us about it." Dixie tore off a paper towel and wiped her face.

"Hey, sunshine, are you okay?" Disco had noticed my tears and moved closer to peer at me through his wire-rimmed glasses.

As he leaned in, I noticed that his shirt, which I'd thought was bright blue with colorful splotches, was instead bright blue with colorful cartoon character French fries dancing all over it.

"I'm fine," I reassured him. "Dixie and I were actually talking about the 'hullabaloo,' as you put it." I patted my eyes again.

"Oh, good. That's good." A big smile spread across his face as he spotted the plate on the counter. He reached out a beringed hand for a scone. "I was afraid maybe somebody else had died."

And my scones are no longer safe.

Dixie reached into one of the drawers and pulled out a small paper bag. "Here you go. Take these back to the store with you."

"Outta sight!" He didn't hesitate at all. Grabbing the bag, he left as quickly as he'd come, taking my afternoon snack with him as he headed out the door.

"At least he'll appreciate them," I said sadly.

"What?" Dixie looked at me.

"The scones." I gave her a sad smile. "At least Disco will appreciate them."

"You whiner." Dixie scoffed. "I saved you some. They're in the back."

I perked up.

With all of our visitors having departed, Dixie and I could get started on our day and focus on our tasks for the morning. Settling into my office chair, I called Mame and left her a message, thinking she might check her voicemail.

I knew I also needed to call Lewis Brimley and tell him about the recipe cards Greer had given me but decided to put it off for a bit longer. I needed to handle it delicately because I was sure he'd want to keep them to review and they weren't mine to hand over. Our planned meeting was scheduled for a couple of days from now, and really, what was the harm in waiting until then?

The morning flew by with, thankfully, no more visitors. Both Dixie and I got a lot accomplished. What with the scones and coffee, I didn't notice it was lunchtime until the back door swung open and Dixie's brother, Hirsh, strolled in.

"Hey, Sugar." He stuck his head in my office. "Is Dixie around?" He was carrying a foil-covered baking dish.

"What have you got there?" Dixie came down the hallway to see who'd arrived, and he handed the dish to her.

"Your mother is sure you're starving to death." He held the baking dish to his chest dramatically. "She has sent provisions." He grinned. "And she made too much enchilada casserole."

"Your mother always makes enough to feed an army,"

Dixie countered. "I'm in trouble because I haven't been by lately, aren't I?"

"Sort of," he said. "And it's kind of my fault because I mentioned talking to you yesterday. And then she said she hadn't seen you in two weeks."

"It hasn't been that long." Dixie rolled her eyes. "But I'll stop by on my way home tonight."

"I know she'd love that." Hirsh smiled.

"I was just thinking about lunch." I stood. "Shall I get plates?"

"That would be great." Dixie took the dish from her brother.

"Three plates or two?" I looked at Hirsh.

"I ate when she was packing up the food." He patted his midsection. "But I'll join you for a few minutes. I'd like to hear what you've decided on the security cameras."

"There's more room out front." I pointed. "Though we really should lock the front door. Unless we want updates on the St. Ignatius soap opera drama, *The Days of Our Pies*. You two go ahead, and I'll bring the plates."

Dixie shook her head, and Hirsh looked at me like I'd lost my mind.

"Come on." She motioned to him. "I'll explain."

I grabbed plates, napkins, and silverware. Plus a scone for Hirsh. See, I wasn't completely selfish with my scones. However, I didn't like to see them wasted on unappreciative nibblers.

Dixie had already started filling Hirsh in on our morning and the excitement at the Red Hen. He laughed but not as much as we had.

I served up some of the casserole for Dixie and me and

handed her a fork. Then I offered Hirsh the plate with the scone.

Dixie looked at me askance. "So you hide the scones from others but Hirsh gets one?"

"Some people are more scone-worthy than others." I sniffed. "I like him."

"Ah, cranberry orange." He snatched it right away.

"See?"

As we ate, we reviewed the security camera options with Hirsh. By the time we finished, we had landed on a very simple camera that had a motion detector that worked with a cell phone. You could turn it on or turn it off. So we could activate it when we left for the day and turn it off when we arrived in the morning. He agreed with the sheriff that we should consider a camera for both front and back.

Hirsh stood. "Let me take this page with me, and I'll see what kind of pricing I can get for you through my company."

"Thanks. That would be great." Dixie began clearing up dishes.

"How are things going with your YAP kids?" I asked. "Did Dixie tell you they brought us a donation jar?"

"She did." He stuck the printout in his pocket. "They're doing pretty well. The auction for the skate park is coming together. The community has been very supportive. And it's been good for the kids to have to talk with people, respect-fully ask for help, and accept no with grace. Many of them don't have that example at home."

"The three we met seemed like nice kids." I smiled, remembering their nervousness. "Awkward, but nice."

"They are good kids," Hirsh agreed. "It's a process."

"And very passionate about skateboarding," I noted. "At least Zac is."

"Yes," he agreed. "He's a bright kid. I wish he'd spend more energy on his studies, but his passion is skateboarding."

"I can see that. When we got him talking about it, he came alive. A place for the kids to go would make him very happy."

"That would be Zac." Hirsh chuckled. "And if we can get something going where they can practice, it will make Terry very happy too. Then the sheriff won't be chasing them off the sidewalk all the time."

Hirsh stopped by the kitchen to say goodbye to Dixie and went out the back.

Back in my office, I moved a stack of papers and began the process of answering emails. A few minutes later, Dixie popped in.

"I'm going to run and grab some of the things I need to try out this one recipe"—she held up the card—"and stop by to see my mother."

"Sounds good." I nodded. "By the way, we have an email that there's an emergency meeting of the merchants' association tonight at six. What do you want to bet that it has something to do with the drama at the Red Hen this morning?"

She sighed. "We'd better be there."

"Do you want to pick me up?" I needed to go home and feed Ernest before then.

"Sure. I'll pick you up at ten minutes 'til."

I went back to responding to emails and clearing out junk mail, happy that the afternoon was quieter than the morning had been. I'd crossed three items off my list and added only two. So that was net progress, right?

Twenty minutes later, I'd taken the opportunity to stand and stretch, as well as refill my coffee cup. I jumped when I heard the chime at the front ding and a voice call, "Hello."

Mame Reinhart still had her lunch lady apron on, and

from the looks of it, lunch had included marinara sauce. In her arms, she had the antique box that had been at Marla's house the day before.

Sliding it onto the counter, she let out a big huff. "Thanks so much for suggesting I return this to Dwayne Darling, Sugar."

I was surprised to see her. I hadn't meant for her to bring it; I had wanted to talk through the idea of returning it with her. "It's great that you want to do that. But there's no big rush, is there?"

"There sort of is because the lawyer is going to send an appraiser to Marla's tomorrow. And I don't think it's worth a lot, but I don't want it as part of the appraisal because it's not mine." She wiped her brow with her apron.

I thought she was splitting hairs, but technically, she was right.

"In that case, you're probably right to do that now." I ran a hand across the carving on the top of the box. It was easier to see the relief here in the light of the big plateglass window.

"But I don't want to do it at all." She shook her head adamantly. "I want you to do it."

"I could go with you," I offered.

"No." She shook her head again. "I don't want to go at all."

"Is he really that scary?" He couldn't be that bad. Maybe kind of a grumpy guy. But Mame's aunt was Mrs. Pickett and Mame dealt with her. That took some gumption.

Her face fell. "I guess not. But, Sugar, I just can't deal with one more thing." Her lip quivered.

That got me. It wouldn't be that much trouble to find out whether the guy wanted the box. If he did, great. If not, I'd take it back to Mame. Or maybe have the ladies at Auntie's Attic take a look at it.

"Okay, I'll take care of it." I sighed, looking at the box with a bit of reluctance. "But it may not be right away. We're trying to get this cookbook done for the band boosters so they'll have it for the Fall Festival, and we have a couple of other irons in the fire."

Her shoulders visibly relaxed, and she gave me a grateful hug. "Thank you, Sugar. I'm sorry to be a bother."

I returned her hug, stepped back, and gave her a smile. "You're not a bother at all, Mame."

Her eyes widened suddenly. "Sorry, I've got to go! I completely forgot. I've got ice cream in the car." She was gone as quickly as she'd come. And I was left with an old wooden box, another task to add to my list, and the feeling that Dixie was right.

I really was a sucker.

15

The merchants' association meeting was in full swing by the time Dixie and I arrived, and it was a full house. Everyone was talking at once, and I didn't think several people in attendance were actually merchants.

Red Hen Diner proprietor Toy George sat up front. In the row behind her, I spotted Lark Travers from Travers Jewelry, Tressa Hostetter from Tressa's Tresses, Harry from the hardware store, Tina Martin, and Disco.

However, looking around, I did not spot any refreshments. No coffee. No delicious slices of pie like there had been at the last merchants' meeting. Shoot.

Guess they didn't want to take the chance of a food fight if things got out of hand. Like this morning.

The producer, a short, spray-tanned guy in designer jeans and a hoodie, along with a handful of others who must have been some of the staffers from the show, was standing in one corner of the room. I couldn't remember the producer's name.

Mayor Kirby was leaning against the wall next to them. I didn't see Dino anywhere, and I had to admit I was relieved.

Dixie and I found chairs in the middle of the room and sat.

Julie Haynes was the chair of the group but wasn't having any luck getting people to quiet down so she could talk. She kept holding up her hand and waving it, but no one even paused. We'd never had a gavel for the group, but we might have needed to invest in one. In the past, the meetings had always been organized and civil.

I was about to lean over and ask Dixie to do her whistle. That lady has an ear-piercing whistle, and I was sure it would interrupt the chatter long enough for Julie to gain control. Suddenly, though, the crowd hushed and heads turned toward the back of the room.

Sheriff Terry had entered along with Officer Butters. Stepping to the side, they didn't take seats but lingered at the back of the room. Their silent entrance had been enough to provide a break for Julie.

"Thank you for coming at such short notice," she began. "While we love having a film crew in town and the opportunity to shine a light on St. Ignatius, it has come to our attention that there have been some problems."

"You better believe there have." Toy George stood up and pointed a finger at the filming group. "Those people showed up, came right in, and started ordering my customers around."

"Wait a minute," the mayor interrupted. "They were only trying to do their job."

"And I was tryin' to do mine." Toy glared at Mayor Kirby. "People come to the Red Hen to eat. Not to look pretty on TV."

Most did, anyway. Smiling to myself, I remembered Tina's elaborate outfit and Disco's French fry shirt.

The producer spoke up. "If we're going to go forward with this project, we have to be able to film at the diner."

"Leo, of course we want you to continue," the mayor was quick to say. Apparently, he was on a first-name basis with the guy.

Toy stood again and opened her mouth to make another comment. From the look on her face, it was not going to be a nice one.

"Let's stop." Julie held up her hand. "We need to come up with a compromise that will allow customers to continue to use the diner and still allow the film crew to get the video they need. Agreed?"

There were a lot of nods around the room.

"When does the actual filming for the episode start?" I asked, looking toward the producer.

"Next week," he responded. "We were trying to grab some footage of the business for a promo spot."

"Could you do that when the diner's closed?" Dixie suggested.

"No, we need people in there," he answered.

"What about early morning right at opening when the place isn't so packed?" I offered. "Toy, would that make it easier?"

"Maybe." She turned to look at me.

"And maybe, Mr. Mostel, the perfect shot isn't so important that you need to shout at customers." Julie directed her comment to the producer.

Leo Mostel. That's the guy's name. I guess I heard it from someone but forgot it.

"For Pete's sake, I didn't understand why the man was shouting." Leo frowned, raising his voice. "I didn't know the guy had hearing issues. I was trying to calm him down."

"Hmm, by yelling?" Dixie said under her breath. "That's an interesting calming technique."

Leo's frown deepened as he looked around the diner. "Look, people, I don't mean to cause a problem. I only want to get good footage for the promo."

"And I only want to not have chaos in my diner," Toy shot back.

I could tell Leo wanted to say more. Possibly point out that it wasn't him or his crew who had thrown a pie. But instead, he took a deep breath and nodded. "Alright. We can start filming early in the morning, first thing when the diner opens. It should be quieter then, and maybe we can get some footage of people coming in."

Toy seemed placated. "If you'll let me know when you're coming, I'll make sure to let people know that things may temporarily be a little off."

I could feel the energy in the room shift.

Julie summed things up to make sure everyone agreed. And she suggested that if the crew were filming in other places around town, the same heads-up would be helpful to those merchants. "Outdoor filming isn't a problem as long as you're not blocking access to someone's business, but if you're going inside, we'd appreciate it if you'd check in with the manager or owner of the place."

Leo nodded and motioned to his crew to exit. As they moved to the door, I saw that Sheriff Terry and Officer Butters had already slipped out without anyone noticing.

Dixie and I exchanged glances. "Ready to go?" she asked.

"More than." I nodded.

We picked up our bags and waved to Toy. Walking back through the diner to get to the door, I noticed several of the film crew in a booth. Katie, one of the waitresses, was taking their orders. I crossed my fingers and hoped that they truly were fans of diner fare because the Red Hen would not disappoint.

Dixie had parked out front, and we made our way to her pickup.

"Would you mind if we stopped by the shop for a minute?" Dixie asked. "I'd like to drop off these things I picked up at the grocery store, and then I won't have to deal with them in the morning."

"No problem. I'm in no rush to get home." Ernest had been fed, and maybe if I was late enough, Mrs. Pickett would be in bed and couldn't accost me.

Dixie pulled into the alley that led to the back of our shop, and just as she did, a figure ran across the alleyway. We both screeched and Dixie slammed on the brakes.

We looked at each other. "Probably a kid taking a shortcut home." She gulped.

"Probably." I agreed, gulping too and waiting for my heart rate to return to normal. "With the break-ins and all, we're on edge."

"Yeah, I guess so." She laughed nervously as she pulled in and parked. "I can run this in." She picked up a couple of grocery bags. "It won't take but a minute."

"I'll go in with you." It may have been a kid cutting through, and there was no reason to think that whoever had opened the window at the shop was coming back. But I'd feel better if we were together.

Unlocking the back door, I then held it open so Dixie could go through with the bags. I flipped on lights as we went.

"None of this needs to be refrigerated, so I'll leave the unpacking for tomorrow." Dixie came out of the kitchen and into the hallway. "What's that?" She pointed.

I'd put the wooden box that Mame had dropped off in the

middle of my desk. "That's the antique box I was telling you about." I explained that Mame had brought it and how she wanted me to take it to Dwayne Darling.

Dixie moved toward the desk for a closer look and ran her fingers across the top. "Nice wood. Interesting carving. Do you really think it's worth anything?"

"I don't know." I shrugged. "Maybe. Maybe not."

"There wasn't anything in it?" She lifted open the hinged lid.

"No, completely empty. Mame thought that Marla had been using it to gather some of the cookbook recipes and that's why she took it to the historical society. But Lewis said it was empty and in the way, so he brought it to Mame. And now the attorney for Marla's estate is sending an appraiser tomorrow, and Mame wanted it out of the house." There was a little more to it, but that was the situation in a nutshell.

"So why didn't she take it to Dwayne? Or call him to come and get it?" Dixie closed the lid.

"She says she's kind of scared of him." I shrugged.

"So she talked you into doing it for her, right?" Dixie gave me a pointed look.

"Maybe."

"You are …"

"I know, a sucker."

"Do you think it's safe here?" she asked.

"It's an empty old box." I ran my fingers over the carving on top. "If the Cash Burglar does show up, I think it'll be fine. Antiques are not his jam."

Dixie nodded. "I guess if he stops by here, he'll find out we've got plenty of dough but not the kind he's looking for." She snickered at her own joke.

I groaned. "Take me home. Before the jokes get worse."

THE NEXT MORNING, IT SEEMED LIKE THE NIGHT HAD BEEN short and the alarm had buzzed way too soon. I was in the kitchen making coffee when Ernest padded in looking as sleepy and confused as I felt.

One cup down, and my attitude was a little better. I'd treated Ernest to a saucer of milk in addition to his usual breakfast kitty kibble. His "cattitude" had not improved.

Taking my second cup of coffee upstairs with me, I tried to remember what I had on my calendar for today and realized I had a free day. Not exactly free, but I could tackle my office and catch up on things I'd been putting off because I didn't have enough of a time block.

All right, now I was motivated. I jumped in the shower and then, wrapping myself in a towel, dried my hair. Jeans with a turtleneck ought to work for an in-office day.

I had gathered my work bag and my purse and was ready to head out the door when my phone rang. I saw that it was Greer.

"Hey, good morning," I answered.

"Have you heard?" Her excitement came through in her voice.

"No, I haven't left the house yet. What's going on?"

"There was another break-in last night on the square, and they've got the Cash Burglar on video!"

"Really? That is exciting. How do—" I started to ask how she knew but stopped myself. It was always somebody's cousin's aunt or some such thing who worked at the sheriff's office.

"Nellie Kaufman's daughter was at the Red Hen just now and heard about it there."

"I hope the video is clear enough that they can see who it is." Some cameras were better than others. One of the details we'd looked at during our own security camera research.

"Oh, it sounds like it," Greer said brightly. "Nellie says that her daughter heard they got a really good shot."

"That will certainly answer a few questions about the break-ins," I said. "And make all of us feel safer."

"I'll let you go, Sugar. I know you're probably anxious to get to work. But I wanted to make sure you had heard."

"I appreciate it, and let me know if you hear anything more."

"I will," Greer promised. "And you do the same."

Even with the delay, I arrived at the office before Dixie. I made coffee and settled in at my desk. I heard the back door open when she arrived and called, "Good morning."

"If you say so." She dropped into the chair beside my desk. I guessed we were all having trouble getting started today. Maybe it was the weather change.

"Bad night?"

"No, a good night. But a bad morning." She rubbed her eyes. "I stopped to get gas and discovered I had a flat tire. I had them keep the truck so they could fix it, but the only one available to give me a ride was that smelly Too-Much-Cologne Barney, who talks all the time." She sighed.

"It was that awful?" I patted her arm.

"I know I should be nicer, but come on, guy. And it's not bad enough that he smells like he soaked in Eau de Pew all night, but he talks nonstop."

"About what?"

"Doesn't matter." She sniffed the arm of her jacket. "Smell this." Holding out her arm for me to take a whiff, she asked, "Do I stink like men's cologne now?"

I shook my head. "No, I don't smell anything."

"Barney has been watching some program about aliens, and now I know everything I'll never need to know about UFOs. Did you know that a bunch of documents were recently declassified and show that the government has been retrieving alien technology from crash sites for years? Some as long as fifty years ago."

"I did not know that." I smiled. "Sorry you had such a crazy morning."

"Sorry to rattle on." She sighed. "How was your morning? I hope better than mine." "I had a call from Greer this morning, and it seems we may not need that security camera, after all." I stood and went to get Dixie some water.

"Why is that?" She took a sip.

"The Cash Burglar has been caught on video, and according to somebody's aunt's cousin, they're hoping for an arrest soon."

"That's great news." Dixie stood.

"It really is," I agreed.

"I still think we should go ahead with the camera, though." She shrugged off her jacket and went to hang it up. "Last night, Hirsh gave me the pricing he could get for us if he ordered them and I told him to go ahead. It'll take two to three weeks, but it wasn't expensive." She gave me the numbers.

"That sounds reasonable." I noted the amount on a pad on my desk. "Let's do it."

"I'll let him know." She searched in her jacket pocket for her phone.

As she moved to the other room, I could hear her talking to her brother. I envied the easy camaraderie they had. As an only child, I had never experienced it.

I was deep into sorting the myriad of papers on my desk, discarding some, filing others, and didn't realize she'd come back. I looked up to see her in the doorway, her brow furrowed, her expression serious.

"What's up?" I hoped it wasn't bad news about one of her parents or her grandmother.

"It seems they do have a decent photo of the Cash Burglar," she said. "And it's one of Hirsh's YAP kids."

"Oh, no." My heart sank. "Which one?" I hoped it wasn't Zac; he'd seemed like such a great kid and so excited about the skate park. In the short encounters we'd had with him, I'd gotten kind of attached to the kid.

"Hirsh wasn't sure, but Terry said the kid clearly had on a "YAP" T-shirt. He'd asked Hirsh to come to the sheriff's office. That's where he was when I called." She frowned. "He said he'd stop by after if he could."

I couldn't believe it. "Whichever kid it was, what were they thinking?" I sat back in my chair. The news had knocked the wind out of my sails.

We both got back to what we'd been working on, and two hours later, we'd not heard from Hirsh.

Finally, when we'd almost given up hope, Dixie's phone buzzed.

"Hirsh?" she answered. "Okay, hold on. I'm standing here with Sugar, and I'm going to put you on speaker." She pushed the button and held the phone so I could hear.

"Sorry I couldn't stop by." He sounded tired. "This took longer than I thought it would, and I've got to get to a work site to deal with a problem. That's where I was heading this morning when Terry called. But never mind all that."

"What about the video?" Dixie asked.

"Unfortunately, there's no good news." He took a deep breath. "I've got bad news and worse news."

"Oh, no." I feared what he was about to say next.

"The person on the video is one of my guys, and it's Zac. Plus, he didn't show up at school today. Terry and I went to the apartment where he lives with his mother. He's not there either."

Dixie and I looked at each other.

"Oh, Hirsh." My stomach twisted. I felt sick for him and sick for Zac. "I hope you and Terry can find him."

"Keep us posted, okay?" Dixie asked.

"I will," he promised. "Catch you later."

16

As hard as I tried, I couldn't get my mind back on work or myself back on task. The news about Zac had really upset me. Did the kid need money? Why cash? Was he into drugs or something? I didn't know how much drugs cost in the rural farm town market, but I would bet the small amounts Sheriff Terry had described wouldn't cover it.

I knew I could be wrong about people, but I still couldn't square the idea of Zac as the Cash Burglar with the interactions we'd had with him. Finally, frustrated and needing something to distract myself, I went in search of Dixie.

"Do you know where this Dwayne Darling guy lives?" I asked.

"Sure. His farm is east of town a little bit. Beyond the sale barn but not as far as the rock quarry. Why?"

"I'm driving myself crazy here. Worrying about things I can't do anything about." I paced while I talked. "I think I'll deliver that box to him. Then I'll at least have accomplished something."

"Do you want me to go with you?" she asked. "I have a

dentist appointment, but I'll gladly cancel." She smiled a big smile.

"Oh, no, you don't." I pointed a finger at her. "You're not going to use me to get out of your dentist appointment. Seriously, I'm fine on my own, but can you write down directions for me?"

"Sure." She grinned. "I don't think your handy-dandy GPS is going to find this one."

∼

ARMED WITH DIXIE'S VERY EXPLICIT DIRECTIONS, I HAD NO trouble finding the place. It sat just off the main gravel road, and the plain gray mailbox had "Darlin Farm" on it. I was sure there'd been a *g* on it originally, but it must have disappeared somewhere along the way.

I pulled into the driveway and up to the weathered farmhouse, the wooden box in my passenger seat. The late afternoon sun was casting long shadows across the overgrown yard, where a rusty tractor was leaning against a pile of wood. Getting out of the car, I went around and picked up the box. I could handle it, but the solid wood made it heavy, and the weight made me think I needed to up my workout game.

The porch steps creaked as I climbed them. I opened the worn screen door and knocked loudly. Then I stepped back and let it swing shut.

"Mr. Darling," I called out.

A curtain twitched at the window, and then the front door groaned open. "What do you want?" he asked through the screen, his voice as rough as the stubble on his chin.

The man was tall with sun-leathered skin and blue eyes that seemed permanently squinted from too many harsh-weather days. He hitched up the strap of his overalls. Clean but faded, they were covering a chambray work shirt.

He didn't speak but raised bushy eyebrows and waited.

"I'm Sugar Calloway, and I work with Dixie Spicer," I explained. "We make community cookbooks."

"Don't need any cookbooks if that's what you're selling." He stepped back as if to close the door.

"Wait," I stopped him. "I'm not selling anything." I held up the box. "I came to return this."

"What is it?" He opened the screen door to look.

"It's an antique box, and I think it may have belonged to your family."

He reached out as if to touch it. A wave of what looked like sadness washed over his face.

"I'm working on a project at the historical society, and Marla Mercer had it there before she died." The words came out in a rush. "And Mame Reinhart said Marla had told her it belonged to your wife, Delores."

The name landed between us like a stone dropped in still water. Dwayne's expression turned hard.

"Anything in it?" He pulled back his hand.

"No, it's empty." I held it out to him. "I guess there were some recipes and things in it that Marla was working with."

Dwayne moved forward, pushing the screen door open wider and stepping outside. "Don't want it."

"But—" I began.

"I said I don't want it, dammit. Take it back to Mame. Or toss it in the creek. I don't care." His voice harsh, he turned to go back inside and then paused and turned. His pale-blue eyes pinned me.

"And tell Mame not to be digging up the past. Some things are better left buried." The screen door banged shut, and the front door slammed with enough force to rattle the windows.

I stood there a few moments, holding the box and watching as dust danced in the sunlight that was cutting across the porch.

Finally, I turned and walked back to my car, sure I was being watched from the window. And very certain that if Mame had been the object of Dwayne Darling's wrath, the lady would have passed out.

As for me, I felt sure the anger was his way of dealing with a monumental hurt. A hurt that, even after ten years, had not healed.

WHEN I GOT BACK TO THE SHOP, I SHOVED THE WOODEN BOX onto a shelf in our storeroom.

So much for getting something accomplished.

"I will deal with you later," I told it. "I thought you'd be the easy and uncomplicated thing to tackle, but no." I pushed it to the back. "Now you'll just have to wait your turn."

"Who are you talking to?" Dixie said from the doorway.

I started and then laughed. "I thought you'd still be at the dentist."

"No. All done." She gave me an exaggerated smile. "How did it go with Dwayne?"

I gave a big sigh.

"You didn't get lost, did you?" She picked up a canister from the shelf beside her and turned to leave.

"No, I found it okay." I sighed again. "But it didn't go well."

I followed her out of the storeroom and into the kitchen. "He did not want the box. Did not want to chat. Told me to throw the box away or give it back to Mame and to tell Mame to let the past stay in the past."

"I guess that answers that." She began measuring flour and dumping it into a mixing bowl. "Was he as scary as Mame said?"

"He wasn't scary. Big and gruff maybe. But I'm glad I went in place of Mame; I think she would have run in terror or passed out."

"I wonder what her story is," Dixie mused. "She seems so timid and nervous."

"She talked about it a little when I was at her house the first time." I tried to see what Dixie was making but couldn't see a recipe card or paper. "It sounds like the thing she, Marla, and DeeDee had in common was the loss of a parent. And it seems like it affected them all differently."

"Losing someone does." Dixie pulled out the olive oil. "Were they all young when that happened?"

"She said Marla lost her mother and ended up taking care of her father. Mame told me Marla was only ten. And then Mame was a little older when her mom died and her dad remarried."

"Must have been the connection to Delores as well." Dixie nodded as she set a garlic clove on the counter. "I remember when she disappeared and all that was the talk of the town. People talked about her parents dying when she was a kid."

"All that gossip about his wife running away might cause a guy to become a hermit." I was thinking that Dwayne, having been through such a rough time, got a bit of a pass on being gruff with people. "That couldn't have been pleasant."

"No. It's the dark side of 'everybody knows everybody's business.'" She paused, pulled out a baking sheet, and flipped on the oven. "When you're going through something, most people care and want to support you. But there are also those who, at a hint of bad news, turn into sharks getting a sniff of scandal." She raised her gaze from the mixing bowl. "Gossip mongers feed on each other and delight in sharing bad news."

It sounded like she was speaking from experience.

"What is it you're making?" I changed the subject.

"Oh, I saw this bread recipe in a magazine when I was at the dentist's office and wanted to try it." A sprig of rosemary had joined the garlic on the counter.

"Of course you did." I smiled. Dixie's never-ending interest in baking and cooking was part of what made her brilliant at it. To her, it was both the science of getting things right and the art of adding your own touches and making it uniquely yours. "I can't wait to try it."

"We'll see how it goes. I'm hoping to up my bread game before I need to test our recipes for the historical society cookbook. What are we calling it?"

"We still need to brainstorm. We don't have a title yet." I'd written some ideas down, but I didn't love any of them. "I'm going to return to my office and see if I can't accomplish something."

"Sounds like a plan."

"Any news on our skateboarder?"

"None."

I went back to sorting in my office and tried to keep my mind on the task at hand, but Zac's situation and where he might have gone was still niggling at the back of my mind.

In a short time, Dixie's bread filled the shop with fragrant goodness. The aroma was warm and delicious. By lunchtime, it was killing me.

I made my way back to the kitchen, where the bread was cooling and Dixie was leaning on the counter, making notes.

"That smells wonderful, and I'm starving. But I don't want to go to the Red Hen and listen to all the chatter about Zac," I said.

"I know." She looked up. "I feel the same way."

"Do we have anything here?"

She rummaged in the pantry and held up a can of tuna. "Would this work?"

"Works for me." I got out the mayo and a bowl. Dixie opened the can, drained the tuna, and began adding her touches.

We had assembled our sandwiches and were about to dig in when the bell out front dinged. I was closest, so I got up to check it out. It was Sheriff Terry.

"How are you doing?" Dixie asked when she saw him following me into the kitchen.

"Not going to lie to you, it's been a rough morning." He rubbed his jaw.

I nodded. "I'll bet."

"Never would've suspected Zac Eaton." He wiped a hand over his haggard face. "I mean, we were always chasing the skateboarders off the sidewalk. But breaking the rules about skating where you shouldn't, that's a long way from breaking and entering."

"No luck with finding him?" Dixie asked.

"None. We've got a BOLO."

Don't ask me how I knew "BOLO" stands for "be on the lookout," but I do. I pushed my plate away, no longer hungry.

"No other family in the area?" I couldn't remember Zac mentioning anyone.

"Only his mom. His dad lives out of state. He could be headed there, but his mom didn't seem to think so. Apparently, the guy is a real piece of work."

"And Zac's friends?" Probably the biggest influence on a teen.

"I talked to his two skateboarding friends, Gil and Bruce, who Hirsh said he hangs with the most." Sheriff Terry shook his head. "Nothing. They all seem like decent kids."

"Hirsh said the same thing." Dixie pushed her plate away too. "And he's been working with the boys for a while."

"Could there have been something Zac needed the money for?" I asked.

"Oh, speaking of money, here's your hundred back. I left the jar out front. Since nothing was taken, we're not putting your open window down as a B & E."

"Fair enough. Nothing was broken, and it doesn't seem like anyone entered." I accepted the hundred-dollar bill. "Still a mystery how it got there though."

"I'll ask Hirsh how we get the money to the skate park fund." Dixie stood and began to pick up dishes. "Though I'm still baffled about where it came from."

The skate park fund.

Dixie and I looked at each other, the light bulb moment hitting us at the same time. "The skate park fund," we said in unison.

"I bet Zach was stealing the cash to add to the skate park fund." It fit what we knew about Zac's passion for skateboarding. Though why he'd decided on the breaking-in-and-stealing-cash route was beyond me.

"That could be it," Sheriff Terry agreed.

"What will happen to him when you catch him?" I asked, fearing I already knew the answers.

"Even if you're right, it's still stealing." Sheriff Terry picked up a slice of the still-warm bread. "Though since he's a minor and has no record of anything before this, he might get off with probation."

"I hope that's the case." I began picking up.

He paused. "If that's all he's done. And I hope it is."

"You don't think ..."

"Maybe not intentionally." His eyes clouded. "But if he surprised Marla and she picked up the knife and they struggled ... Fear can make people make bad choices."

He let the thought hang in the air.

A sick feeling settled in my stomach.

And it didn't leave me for the rest of the day.

17

After a sleepless night, the sick feeling hadn't left me. After the discussion with Sheriff Terry yesterday, it seemed to have taken up permanent residence. I couldn't get Zac out of my mind. I made my way to the shop, which usually perked me up, but not today. Even my morning coffee was unappealing. I spent the morning preparing for my upcoming meeting with Lewis Brimley about the historical society cookbook.

Dixie and I had sorted out the potential recipes for inclusion. I'd decided that the only way to deal with the recipe cards Greer had given me was to make copies and show them to Lewis, not take the actual cards. That way, I could safely return the cards to Bunny and still let Lewis go over the recipes we wanted to use to fill in the gaps. I had tried taking photos of the cards with my phone, but the clarity wasn't great and I'd have to print them for Lewis anyway.

We had a copier in the shop, but our little printer didn't do anything else. It only printed, with no scanning or copying abilities. The office supply store on the other side of the square had larger multifunction copiers I could use, so I decided to take advantage of their services.

I let Dixie know I was leaving and would be back in a few.

Because I didn't have meetings, I'd dressed in work-at-the-office jeans and my cheeky "IOWA (75% vowels, 100% awesome)" T-shirt. Checking the outside temperature before heading out, I grabbed the light jacket I'd brought from home and stuffed my wallet and the cards in a pocket.

The office supply store wasn't far, and I enjoyed the walk. The courthouse as a centerpiece and the shops that surrounded it always delighted me. Java Junction, the new coffee shop Max had mentioned, was decked out like a train station with antique railway train ticket office memorabilia.

Maybe I'd pick up a coffee on my way back.

Many of the shops had posters promoting the upcoming Fall Festival in their windows, which reminded me we needed to put ours up.

As I stepped inside the office supply store, I pulled the yellowed recipe cards out of my pocket and went to check out the copiers.

On my way to the area at the back where the machines were, I noticed Racine from the historical society and suddenly remembered the morning I'd seen her with Zac. I wondered how close they were and whether she'd maybe heard from him.

"Hey, Racine." I approached her casually. "How are you? I've been hoping I could get in on a tour one of these days."

"Oh, hi." She picked up a packet of pens and then put them down. "I'll have one with a high school group coming up soon. If you wouldn't mind tagging along on that, I could get you in."

"I wouldn't mind at all. I left my info with the ladies who

were at the front desk, but I can give it to you directly." I pulled a business card from my wallet.

"No, that's okay. I'll get it from them." She picked up some markers.

"Here, take this anyway." I tucked the card into the front pocket of her purse. "Speaking of high school, do you know Zac Eaton?"

"Not really," she hedged. "I mean, I've heard of him, of course. You know …" She looked up at me, but then her gaze slid away.

Again, the town grapevine was faster than the fastest internet fiber, so without a doubt, practically everyone in St. Ignatius, including Racine, had heard that Zac was being looked at as the culprit in the break-ins.

I stared at her, and she squirmed. "Racine, I saw you two talking the last time I was at the historical complex. And it sure looked like, at the very least, that you're friends," I pressed.

Her eyes widened, and she fidgeted with the shoulder strap of her purse. "I do know Zac, but I don't know where he is," she blurted out quickly, avoiding eye contact.

Interesting. She'd answered a question I hadn't asked. In fact, all I had asked was whether she knew him. Not whether she knew where he was.

"I really wish, if he's still in town, that he would talk to the sheriff or even to Hirsh Spicer." Maybe if she were in contact with him, she'd pass along the message. "They will eventually find him, but things would go a lot better if he turned himself in."

I touched her arm, and she looked up at me, panic clear on her face.

"Right now, he's only wanted as a suspect in the break-ins,"

I continued. "But they're still investigating Marla Mercer's murder, and I'd hate for them to think he had something to do with that."

"What?" Her hand flew to her mouth. "He didn't—he wouldn't." She stopped, perhaps realizing she'd admitted too much about how well she knew Zac.

"If you do happen to see him, you might share that with him," I pressed my point.

"For sure," Racine said, her voice slightly unsteady. "I hope they find him soon."

She put down the markers she was still holding and slipped out the door.

Moving to the machines, I swiped my credit card, made two copies of the recipe cards, and headed back. The order line at Java Junction was long, so I didn't stop. I would make it a point to go by another day.

Back at the shop, I told Dixie about my encounter with Racine.

"I don't know her." Dixie was making notes on some of the recipes we were reviewing. "Or at least I don't think so."

"Clearly, she knows more than she would admit to." I slid my copies into a folder and set aside the ones I would take to my meeting with Lewis. "We'll see if I hear from her."

I sincerely hoped she had taken what I'd said seriously and shared the advice with Zac.

Dixie had some errands to run, so I settled into my work on the tearoom project and the endless job of reorganizing the files. I was on the floor trying to find the folder I'd dropped when my phone buzzed. I almost let it go to voice-mail, but something made me get up to check the screen. Racine. I'd hoped to stir something up with my comments to her, but I hadn't expected anything so quickly. Hopefully, she had some information for me. Or rather, Sheriff Terry.

"Hello?"

A pause, then a young male voice. "Is this Sugar?"

"It is." I pressed the phone closer to my ear. Background noises made it sound like he was outside. "Who is this?"

"It's Zac." He cleared his throat. "You know, uhm, we talked about skateboarding." His voice pitched up at the end, nervous.

My heartbeat kicked up a notch. I hadn't expected him to call me. I'd hoped Racine would encourage him to call the sheriff.

"Zac, I can see you're calling from Racine's phone. Is she there?" I tried to keep my voice neutral. I was in Zac's corner, but I didn't want to put Racine in any danger.

"No. She let me borrow it. I ditched my phone because I thought the cops might be tracking it."

Smart kid.

Or paranoid.

Or both.

"Listen, I don't want to get Racine into any trouble, but she said I should talk to you. That you said I should turn myself in."

"That's right."

He exhaled hard enough that it sounded like static. "I know how it looks. The break-in. But it's not. I didn't—" He stopped and then started again. "I need to explain some stuff."

I leaned against my desk, my mind racing. Sheriff Terry would have my head if he knew I was talking to his prime suspect instead of calling him immediately, but there was something in Zac's voice. Fear maybe, but not the kind that came from guilt.

"You want to turn yourself in?" I asked.

"Yes." He gulped. "But I need someone to hear me out." A car horn blared in the background. "Someone who will make sure I have a chance."

"Where are you now?" I asked.

He hesitated for a moment before deciding to trust me. "At the historical society."

"Come to the shop," I said, decision made. "Back door, not the front. I'll listen, Zac, but I'm not making any promises. And make sure you get Racine's phone back to her."

"Okay."

"If you were breaking into places, you're still going to have consequences to face."

"I know." His voice dropped. "But there's more to it. And I didn't do anything to the lady at the history place where Racine works. I swear." His voice rose. Real fear came through. "I was there and heard her and a guy talking, and then they were yelling. And I took off."

The hair on the back of my neck stood up. Sheriff Terry needed to hear this, and I didn't want to spook Zac and have him disappear again.

"Okay. Thirty minutes," I said. "And Zac? Don't take any detours."

"Thanks, Sugar." Relief flooded his voice. "I'm on my way."

After we hung up, I stared at my phone, wondering whether I'd made a terrible mistake.

Dixie came in the back door while I was still standing there running various scenarios through my head. I filled her in, and in a matter of minutes, we came up with a plan. She would call Hirsh and see whether he could come. She and Hirsh would hide in the back room, listening while I talked with Zac. If I could convince Zac to turn himself in, Hirsh would take him to talk to Sheriff Terry. The plan seemed solid.

Thirty minutes didn't give us a lot of time, but Hirsh arrived quickly, and by the time I heard a knock at the back, Dixie and Hirsh were in place, hidden in the storeroom.

I quickly moved to the back door and opened it to—Disco.

Oh, no.

Paisley pink shirt, bell-bottom jeans, love beads around his neck. He gave me a big smile.

"What are you doing here?" I waved him away.

He took a step back. "Whoa."

"You need to go!" I gave him a little push.

"Why?" His eyes peered down at me from under his shaggy bangs. "Dude, what's up?"

This is not working.

Disco's laid-back attitude was usually what I loved about him, but he was about to mess up our plans.

Finally, I grabbed his paisley-clad arm and dragged him inside. "Get in here quick."

I looked around before closing the door but didn't see Zac anywhere. I quickly shut the door behind us and shoved Disco down the hallway toward the storeroom.

"What're we hiding from?" Disco asked. "Is somebody after us? Is there an alien invasion? Dude at the car place knows a lot about UFOs, and he was telling me the feds have been hiding evidence of ..."

"Just get in there," I ordered. "Hirsh and Dixie will explain."

I heard the low murmur of voices and hoped they'd get through the explanations before Zac arrived. I looked at my watch. On the nose. He should have been here any minute.

I waited, and fifteen minutes passed. And then another fifteen.

By the time it was half past, three things were very clear.

One: Thirty minutes was too long for Dixie, Hirsh, and Disco to hang out in a small space like the storeroom. They were not good at being quiet. In fact, I could hear enough to know they had devolved into telling knock-knock jokes to pass the time.

Two: I was very bad at arranging clandestine meetings.

And three: Zac was not coming.

After wondering what to do now, I went to the storeroom and told the three jokers the bad news.

The only thing left to do was the right thing—and what I should have done when I first talked to Racine and realized she knew where Zac was.

I should have called Sheriff Terry.

After trying to convince Hirsh to make the call and then pleading with Dixie, I called him myself and fessed up to the whole mess.

"Sugar, I know you think he's a nice kid and all, but that was a big risk."

"I had Hirsh and Dixie as backup," I rationalized. "I was going to talk to him, hear him out, have him talk to Hirsh, who he trusts, and then call you."

"Now—" he began.

"I know." I felt a catch in my throat. "You don't have to tell me. Now he may be harder to find."

"That's right." He wasn't angry. In fact, his voice was quiet and calm, which made me feel worse. "I'm going to have to talk to Racine Middlebrooks and see what I can get out of her."

"I know." I swallowed hard, my heart sinking at how much harder I might have made things.

"Listen, Sugar." He sighed a big sigh. "I know that you meant well. But next time, just call me please."

I pushed the disconnect button and turned to look at the three who were watching me from the doorway.

"How much trouble are you in?" Dixie asked.

"A lot."

∼

THE NEXT MORNING, I WAS STILL STRUGGLING WITH THE POOR choice I'd made the day before in trying to help Zac. I wondered whether the sheriff had been able to talk to Racine and what she'd told him. He was not likely to call me up and let me know. I feared I was reduced to being reliant on the Greer or Tina grapevine for updates.

Since I was going directly to my meeting with Lewis, I had packed up and brought home the materials I would need. Folders with recipes, copies of the recipes from Bunny (I'd kept copies for myself), and some notes I'd made on where we were on the timeline.

He'd wanted to meet at the historical complex. And though it seemed like overkill to me, we were to meet in the boardroom where they had their board meetings. If that's what he wanted to do, so be it.

I'd pulled a pleated navy skirt from my corporate days out of my closet and paired it with a gray sweater, some pearls, and navy pumps. Oh, boy. My mama and my aunts would have been proud. However, at the historical complex, the wind was not my friend as I tried to hold down my skirt with one hand and hang on to my folders with the other. And the heels? Not a good choice; they sank into the soft ground I had to walk across to get to the cinder path leading to the front of the building.

"Good morning," I said, blowing through the door. The same two ladies from my last visit were standing behind the reception desk again.

"Morning," the taller of the two greeted me. "Judy," her name tag said.

Thank goodness for name tags. With the way things had been going lately, I was lucky if I could remember my own name.

"Here to see Lewis?" the other one—Lorraine, according to her tag–asked.

I nodded. "Yes, I am."

"He's in the boardroom," Lorraine continued. "But he said not to disturb him until nine-thirty." There might have been a slight eye roll and an emphasis on "disturb" when she said it.

"No problem. I can wait." I took a seat in the waiting area and put my folders on one of the chairs next to me. "I'm kind of early."

"Would you like a coffee?" Judy tipped her head toward the coffee pot atop a nearby filing cabinet.

"I'd love one." I smiled. "Black is fine."

She poured a cup and came out from behind the desk to bring it to me. "What are these, then?" she asked, pointing to the open folder I was looking through. "Recipes for the cookbook?"

"They are." I handed her the folder so she could see better.

Lorraine came out from behind the desk to look too. Soon they were sitting next to me, discussing the recipes.

"I was noticing the antique coffee pot over there." I pointed. There was a blue-speckled granite coffee pot on display by the modern, working coffee pot. "That's the kind of addition or prop we look for to add to the photos we do of the food. In this case, of the breads."

"That's interesting." Lorraine looked back at the folder of recipes. "I never thought about what you have to do to take pictures of the food. I guess it's not just a slice of bread on a plate."

"You both know what kind of things are in the collections here. Do you have any ideas for historic kitchen or dining pieces that might work with some of these recipes?"

My question opened the floodgates; those two had lots of ideas. I grabbed a pen from my bag and a blank sheet of paper from my notebook and made notes as fast as I could. Antique cutting boards, crockery, linens, cutlery. All great ideas.

An idea was forming in my head. Maybe Max and I could do a walk-through and look at some of the items they were suggesting. Max would have a better eye for what would work best for the photos. And then I could see whether we could arrange to borrow any items he thought might work.

Depending on whether Racine was still speaking to me or not, I had that tour she was going to add me to. Maybe Max could arrange to come along.

"Oh, gosh." Lorraine looked up at the clock. "Now it's after nine-thirty, and we've made you late." She shared a look with Judy.

"Go on back." Judy clambered to her feet and pointed to the hallway. "Sorry about talking your ear off."

"No worries," I told them. "The ideas you've given me will be very helpful."

I gathered up my folders and headed down the hall. I tapped on the door of the boardroom, balancing the cup of coffee the ladies had refilled plus the folders and the notes I'd made with their suggestions.

"Come in, come in," Lewis called.

I elbowed the door open, and Lewis rose from the seat at the head of the mahogany table with a smile. His silver hair was neatly combed, his suit and tie were sharp, and a small St. Ignatius flag pin was decorating his lapel.

"Sugar, my dear. What a welcome sight on this windy autumn morning." He moved from the end of the table to help with my load. Taking my coffee with one hand, he pulled out a chair for me with the other. "I see the ladies out front have taken care of you with a warm beverage."

"They did, and they were very helpful in talking with me about items that might work well in some of the photos we'll want to include."

"I see." The charm slipped for a moment, and a brief flicker of irritation passed over his face as he returned to his seat. "I'm sure they're full of ideas, those two. I can take a look at their suggestions and see what's appropriate."

I should not have mentioned my discussion with the ladies. I'd forgotten how into the details Lewis liked to be. And how he didn't like surprises.

"We can go over them today, or I can include them in my next report. Your choice. And there's something else I'd like to discuss with you."

You're not going to like this surprise either.

"I can review them today. I'm pretty fast." He winked. The charm was back, and I figured, in for a penny, in for a pound.

"As you know, we have the eighteen recipes from Marla's initial group that you gave me last week."

"Eighteen and a half." He smiled, rubbing his chin. "Were you able to figure out anything with the half one?"

"Dixie was able to sort that one out." I wasn't going to bring up Mame and the papers; it seemed like more of a distraction than we needed. "And my friend and landlady, Greer Gooder, shared with me these recipes that were considered years ago when they discussed this kind of a book before."

I handed him the sheaf of papers.

"She had these recipes all this time?" He reached into his pocket for his reading glasses and perched them on his nose.

"One of the committee members had kept them."

"And you think we need these to supplement what we have?" He perused the pages. "Are they any good?"

"Dixie is trying one of them today, and she believes there are several in the group that would be great additions to the cookbook. However, it's up to you."

"You and Dixie are the cookbook experts. If you two think they will help, then I'm all for considering them." He handed the papers back with a smile, his blue eyes crinkling at the corners.

"Great. I'll let you know which ones we're recommending next week."

"Or call me anytime in between." He tapped the desk absently. "You can always pop over to the tax office if you need to check in. However, this is not my busy time of year, so sometimes I'm not there until midmorning. You might want to call ahead."

"I'll do that. Oh, and here's that list of historic kitchen or dining items that Lorraine and Judy suggested might work for our photo shoot." I handed him the notes I'd made. "If you can read my handwriting."

"Your handwriting is lovely." He looked over his readers at me. "These will be in the photos, you say. Which ones?"

"We'd leave that up to Max. Max Windsor is our photographer. Dixie makes the dishes, and Max stages them for the photos. I like to have some items available to him and then give him free rein on what to use."

A concept you'd not be familiar with, Mr. Micromanager.

It was a good thing people couldn't hear my thoughts.

He folded up his reading glasses and put them back in his pocket. "And so, it sounds like, in spite of the delay, we're on track."

I bristled inside at the idea that Marla's death had been a "delay." I hadn't known her that well. Though I felt like I was getting to know her bit by bit through Mame. But seriously, a woman had died.

I tamped down my irritation. Different personalities dealt with things in different ways. As Dixie frequently told me, I was all people all the time. And I guessed, by contrast, Lewis was all dates and numbers all the time.

"Yes, I think it's coming together nicely. In spite of the delay." I smiled thinly.

"On that note, taking a bit of a turn here …" He paused for a moment. "I understand they have identified a young man."

"Yes. Zac Eaton." My stomach tightened.

"Do you know him?"

"Only slightly. He has been working on the skate park project with Dixie's brother." I couldn't keep the tension from my voice. "He seems like a nice kid. Who's had a rough life."

"But apparently a thief," Lewis pronounced, tapping his lip. Again, no compassion. Everything black and white.

"It looks that way."

"And apparently also suspected of Marla's murder."

"Perhaps." I frowned at his immediate jump to associate the two.

"It seems reasonable that he didn't expect anyone to be at the farmhouse and when he broke in and Marla was there …"

Lewis didn't complete the sentence, but I knew where he was going. He wasn't the only one in town who had voiced that possibility. The cards were not stacked in Zac's favor in the court of public opinion.

"I understand that Zac heard somebody arguing with Marla," I shot back. "A man, he says. So though he may be guilty of taking money, I wouldn't be so quick to brand him a murderer."

"Really?" Lewis tapped his pen on his chin thoughtfully. "Well, that's news to me."

I'd said too much. I'd known it as soon as it was out of my mouth. Sheriff Terry was not going to be happy when this bit of information showed up out there on the St. Ignatius Information Superhighway.

"Sorry. I shouldn't have shared that," I said ruefully. "But we all need to be careful about jumping to conclusions when there may be more to the story."

"Indeed, we do." Lewis nodded. "Indeed, we do."

We finished up our meeting, and Lewis asked for the printouts of the recipes Greer had given me, as I thought he might.

"You don't mind if I take some time to review these more thoroughly, do you?" he asked, holding the door for me. "You and Dixie can still provide your recommendations."

"Not at all." I smiled at my accurate assessment of how this meeting would go. "Let me know if you have any concerns once you finish looking at them."

I packed up my things and said my goodbyes, waving to Lorraine and Judy as I went out the door.

Ha. This isn't my first rodeo, Mr. Brimley. I've dealt with control freaks like you before, and I've got your number.

THE WIND HAD DIED DOWN SOME AND I HAD NOTHING WAITING for me at the shop, so I decided to stop by and visit Greer. Now that I had copies of them, I wanted to return the original recipe cards Greer had given me. There was no use taking a chance that they might get mixed in with the other cards and documents.

Though she lived in a retirement village, Greer was not exactly sitting in her rocking chair knitting, so I called first to make sure she was home.

She was one busy octogenarian, and I never knew whether she'd be home, at the community center playing cards, or off on a jaunt somewhere else. Last month, her little group had decided they wanted to go see the world's largest popcorn ball in Sac City. I'd heard it was impressive.

Greer confirmed that she'd be home, so I turned my car toward The Good Life.

I parked and made my way to Greer's unit. Walking was easier than it had been at the historical complex as everything was paved. As I got closer, I could see that Greer wasn't out front on the patio today.

Her patio decorations were all intact. She must have anchored them well. I wondered who my neighbor's blow-up jack-o'-lantern was visiting today. Hopefully, not Mrs. Pickett again. I hadn't noticed whether they'd gotten him tied down any better, but I hoped so.

I knocked on Greer's door, and she called, "Come on in."

Stepping inside, I got a friendly hello and then oohs and aahs over my outfit from the three ladies parked on her sofa. They looked like they'd stopped by for tea and a chat.

"Greer is in the kitchen," Bunny spoke up.

I recognized Bunny, Freda, and Nellie from previous shenanigans they'd been involved in with Greer. Frenchie was in Greer's chair, apparently holding the space for her dog mom, but she gave me a soft "Hello" bark.

"I'm sorry." I stopped, noticing the food items in their laps. "I didn't realize Greer had company."

"Oh, we're not company," protested Nellie. "We're here helping Greer."

"That's right." Freda nodded vigorously.

I held my breath and hoped she'd stop, as her wig had been known to fly off from time to time.

"What are you helping her with?" It seemed to me that Greer was the only one moving around and they were sitting and drinking tea.

"Her pantry." Bunny spoke up from Greer's wingback chair, which seemed to have swallowed her tiny frame. "She's cleaning out her pantry."

I stepped into the kitchen, which, in truth, was about only two steps away in the compact unit. Greer was pulling some warm biscuits from the oven.

"Wow, look at you." She smiled, her cheeks a bright pink from the heat of the oven. "So that's what the ladies were oohing and aahing over?"

Well, I guessed I really needed to up my casual attire game. If a simple skirt and sweater drew this much acclaim, it made me wonder what people must think about my usual fashion sense. Or lack of it.

"I hear your friends out there are 'helping' you clean out your pantry?" I looked around at her pantry door, which stood open, and gave her a questioning look.

Greer shrugged. "I started cleaning it out. You don't want expired stuff taking up room in a little pantry. And there are things that aren't expired yet but I'm not going to use." She held up a can of beets and made a face. "So I called Bunny, Freda, and Nellie and told them to come on over and see if they wanted any of it."

I looked back at the three in the living room and the variety of grocery items on their laps. They all smiled. Nellie held up her box of heart-shaped Love Pasta for me to see. Bunny seemed a little buried in her treasure trove of Protein Wafer Crisps. I hoped her teeth could take it. And with the pile Freda had, she was going to need help getting up.

"At the back of one shelf, we found this biscuit mix I'd never used. It's supposed to taste like the ones you get at that restaurant."

The three in the other room made yummy sounds. Whatever Greer was baking did smell wonderful.

"But the expiration date is in two days, so we decided to cook them." While Greer was talking, she dumped the fresh-out-of-the-oven biscuits into a dish towel-lined basket. "Want one?"

I snagged one and then carried the basket in to the ladies, holding it so they could help themselves without getting up before sitting down myself.

"So why are you all dressed up?" Greer asked, picking up Frenchie so she could reclaim her chair and join the group.

"I had a meeting with Lewis Brimley at the historical complex and thought I should look professional."

"I wouldn't dress up for that guy," Nellie declared.

"I would," Bunny disagreed, munching on her biscuit. "I think he's kind of cute."

"He's way too young for you," Freda commented, shaking her head and grabbing another biscuit. "Besides, he's cheap."

"How do you know?" Bunny glared at the other woman. "Did you date him?"

"No," Freda patted her fake hair with her non-biscuit hand. "He's not my type. But I heard."

Hoping to change the trajectory of where this conversation was headed, I wiped my hands on a napkin and pulled the packet of recipe cards out of my bag.

"I stopped by because I wanted to return these." I extended the cards to Bunny. "Thank you so much for letting us borrow them. They were very helpful."

"Glad to help." Bunny reached for them and then, looking at the butter and crumbs on her hands, indicated I should put them on the table beside her. "Can't believe I still had them."

"I can," Nellie muttered under her breath. "I can't believe you could find them."

As entertaining as the company was, I did need to get to the shop. The band boosters' cookbook had come back from our graphic designer and I needed to look at the proofs. And hopefully, get it off to the printer. They were hoping to have it for sale at the Fall Festival. It was too bad the historical society's cookbook wasn't further along because the festival would have been a good market for it. But they hadn't started it in time.

And then there was the "delay," as Lewis called Marla's murder.

"Ladies, I need to take off." I stood. "It's been a pleasure. Enjoy your tea and your groceries."

I took the now-empty basket to the kitchen and noticed all the food still out on the counter.

"Greer, do you need any help putting things back?" I stepped back into the living room to ask.

Greer's phone must have buzzed because she was holding

it to her ear. "Wait," she mouthed, holding up a finger for silence.

No need; the group had gone quiet.

"Wow," she said to the caller, "that really is something." She paused, listening. "Okay, hon, you take care. Thanks."

She hung up, put her phone down, and took a deep breath.

We all—the ladies, Frenchie, and I—waited for her to tell us about the call.

Greer took another deep breath. "They have arrested that boy. The one they caught on the security camera. Found him scooting along on his skateboard and took him in."

"Whew, I guess we can rest easy now," Freda said.

Greer responded. "Maybe."

And then they all started talking at once.

I swallowed past the lump in my throat.

So they arrested Zac.

Who knew where he'd been headed. I hoped it had been to turn himself in.

I touched Greer's arm to get her attention.

"I need to go."

She nodded and patted my hand.

I let myself out and trudged slowly back to my car.

BACK AT THE SHOP, DIXIE WAS IN THE KITCHEN, ELBOW-DEEP IN flour. She was alone, but I could tell as soon as I saw her face that she knew.

"Tina stopped by?"

She nodded, continuing to knead the dough.

"I was at Greer's returning the recipe cards when she got a phone call." There was more to the Greer visit, but I wasn't going to go into that right now. "The lady has serious contacts."

Walking into my office, I dropped my bag on the desk with a thud. Slumping into my chair, I kicked off my shoes and put my head down. It wasn't long before I heard Dixie wander in and drop into the side chair.

"Done with your bread?" I raised my head.

"It's proofing." She shrugged.

"How long does that take?" I knew nothing about baking bread. Luckily, the supermarket had always been there for me.

"A couple of hours for the first proof."

"You have to do it twice?"

"So many questions." She gave a slight smile. "You let it rise once. Then you punch it down and shape it, but much of the air is knocked out of it when you shape it, so you let it rise again before you bake it."

"I feel like the air has been knocked out of me." I put my head back down.

"I know you do." She put her hand on my shoulder. "Come on and help me in the kitchen." She pulled me out of my chair and then stopped and looked me up and down. "Good golly, Sugar, you don't look dressed for kitchen work with your sweater and pearls. Unless you're trying for one of those celebrity chef fancy bakers."

"You too? Everybody's got an opinion about my clothes today. And don't get me started on celebrity chefs." I blew out a breath. "When is it they're filming the Dino Diner episode at the Red Hen?"

"That's tomorrow. Did you want to go and watch?"

"No. I was asking because I wanted to be sure *not* to be there."

We headed to the kitchen, and Dixie was rummaging in

the cabinets, looking for an apron, when her phone buzzed. It was a text. She picked it up to look.

"The sheriff says our front door is locked," she read the text.

"It is? Should I go check on it?" I started toward the front.

"No need." She stopped me. "I know it's locked."

"How do you know?"

"Because I locked it." She looked back at her phone. "After Tina left, I was afraid it was going to be a steady stream of people wanting to talk about the break-ins—and Zac—and I wasn't up to it. So I locked the door."

"You are a smart cookie." I smiled at her. "Does the sheriff want to talk to us?"

"I told him to come around to the back."

A few minutes later, we heard a knock at the back. Dixie opened the door to let Sheriff Terry in.

"Dixie, Sugar," he greeted us, his expression a mixture of weariness and sadness.

Dixie and I exchanged glances.

"So Zac has been arrested?" I asked, even though I knew the answer. "How did you find him?"

"We didn't, really." The sheriff's brow creased. "He was on his board, skating down the street. Sort of like, 'Here I am.'"

"And he admitted to the break-ins?" I asked.

"Some of them but not all." He rubbed a spot between his brows. "Can we sit?"

"Sure." Dixie motioned. "Come on in the kitchen. I need to check the proofing anyway. And I bet neither of you would turn down a coffee."

"Coffee would be fantastic." I followed her and Sheriff Terry to the kitchen. "Which ones does Zac say he didn't have a hand in?"

"The last few. Says he took the cash before." He paused. "You two were on the right track as far as motive goes. He'd take it and then drop it in one of the donation jars. It was such a small amount, it didn't draw anyone's attention."

"What about our hundred-dollar bill?" Dixie asked. "Was that him?"

"He says no, that wasn't him."

"It's puzzling," I noted. "That morning, it wasn't like we had a lot of people in and out."

"Also," Sheriff Terry continued. "The break-in at Marla's house. He claims that wasn't him either."

"What about our window?" I wondered whether he'd tried and gotten interrupted. Or changed his mind.

Dixie slid two cups of hot coffee onto the counter, and Sheriff Terry and I each took one.

"He doesn't know anything about that. He targeted places where he knows they keep small amounts of cash. Usually, petty cash funds. But he left alone any of the places whose owners were supporting the skate park. Like your shop, the Red Hen Diner, and Travers Jewelry."

Dixie checked her bowl and then rejoined the conversation. "Honor among thieves, huh?"

I frowned, trying to put the pieces of the puzzle together. "What did he say about Marla?"

The sheriff sighed. "Zac claims he was at the historical complex the morning Marla died. And at the farmhouse. He had opened a window intending to go through it, but then he heard voices. A man and a woman arguing. And he got scared and took off."

"Do you believe him?" I took a sip of coffee and waited for the sheriff's response.

"I do." Sheriff Terry took a swallow of his coffee. "He

admitted to the break-ins, and what he's told us matches with what we know about them. But the story about Marla and this unknown man has some problems. Some things don't add up."

I nodded, thinking about Zac and his excitement over the skate park and now him sitting in a cell.

"What will happen to him?"

"For right now, we're looking at breaking and entering. And theft. He is a juvenile and has never been in trouble before, but ..." His voice trailed off.

"Is there anyone who saw him that morning?" I crossed my arms, thinking of that day.

"Are you thinking Racine?" Dixie asked.

"I am," I admitted. "If you remember, when I arrived at the historical society that morning and found Marla, Racine was already there."

"That's right." The sheriff placed his now-empty cup on the counter. "Maybe I'd better have another talk with her." He turned to go.

After Sheriff Terry left, Dixie continued with the recipe she was working on and I headed back to my office to catch up on emails.

I could not see the young man we'd talked to, who was so excited about his fakie frontside, whatever that was, getting into a struggle with Marla Mercer.

The idea that he'd overheard an argument, gotten freaked out, and taken off sat better with my idea of how he might act.

But if that were the case, who was the mystery man, and what was it he and Marla had been arguing about?

18

It was the morning of the filming of the Dino Diner episode at the Red Hen Diner, and it seemed like half the town was on that corner of the square. The residents of St. Ignatius and probably some from the next town over had turned out. Some were curious about the filming and caught up in the excitement. Some were hoping to be extras in the shots. Some were just your routine gawkers.

I hoped Sheriff Terry had staffed up for the day. It did look like they'd blocked off the street in front of the diner, which was good because the crowd was packing the sidewalk in front of the diner and spilling out over the curb and onto the street.

Dixie and I had decided to forego the excitement and try to get some work done. Now that the *Tasty Notes Cookbook* was off to the printer, we needed to make the final selections for the historical society's book's content and get the ball rolling on that.

Even if Lewis had opinions on those recipes from Bunny that I'd left with him, I figured I could convince him to use the ones Dixie had picked. Somehow, I doubted he was really that into the recipes. In my encounters with him, I'd concluded he was mostly interested in control.

Max was planning to stop by. Like Dixie and me, he also wasn't that into the Dino Diner filming hoopla. It would give us a chance to talk through the book's concept. Breads, history, family. What was our overarching theme?

Dixie and I had spread the recipes out on the front counter, placing them back in their categories again: Breads Through History, Basic Breads, Sweet Breads, Rolls and Muffins, and Family Favorites. I placed a sticky note on top of each pile and was counting how many we had in each stack when I heard Max come in the back.

"Look at this sourdough recipe." I pushed a card toward Dixie. "It's got a note about using a starter that's been passed down for five generations in the Trainer family."

"I love it." She handed it back to me and picked up another one. "Depression Cornbread," she read. "The note says it kept the Shaklee family from starving during the Depression."

"Let's move those to the Family Favorites category." I slid them onto that pile. "We're still short on recipes there, and maybe we can rename it to a title that would include recipes like those."

I felt Max come up beside me and leaned into his side. He was solid—and not only in the physical sense. Reliable, honest, straightforward. He took a lock of my hair that had fallen forward while Dixie and I were working and tucked it behind my ear.

"Good morning. It looks like you two are hard at work." He had his camera bag slung over his shoulder even though we weren't taking photos today. As I'd gotten to know Max better, I'd come to understand it was a part of him.

I turned to greet him.

"Uh-oh. What's wrong?" I touched his arm. Though his morning salutation had been light and teasing, his face was serious, his blue eyes troubled.

He paused, setting his camera bag on the floor. "On my way in, I got a call from Terry."

"Yes?" This did not sound good.

"And he and a couple of the deputies are out at Dwayne Darling's farm right now."

"Is Dwayne okay?" I searched Max's face.

"Was he firing his shotgun at trespassers again?" Dixie asked.

Max shook his head grimly. "They got an anonymous tip about a body in an abandoned well on his property. The state crime lab techs can't get there right away, and Terry would like me to grab some photos before anything gets disturbed."

"A body?" I shivered. "Recent?"

"I don't know the details yet," Max said, slipping into his photojournalist voice. "But from what I could gather, he thinks it's been there a while."

Dixie's eyes widened, and she grabbed my arm. "A while? Like ten years?"

I felt my skin prickle. "Is it possible Delores Darling didn't leave town?"

"Didn't they look for her back then?" Max asked Dixie. He and I were both newcomers and neither of us had even heard the story of her disappearance until recently.

"Not really." Dixie let go of my arm and picked up some of the recipe cards from the counter, absently stacking and restacking them.

"They didn't try to find her?" I couldn't imagine there hadn't been a search.

"She left a note, according to Dwayne. Cleaned out his bank account. Was having an affair, left him, ran off with the guy," Dixie explained.

I tapped the batch of recipe cards I was holding on the counter. "Mame said that her friends thought she'd gotten busy with her real estate business, but when it turned out she'd been having an affair, they figured that was why she'd been scarce."

"Maybe she was having an affair but never made it to meet whoever it was she was planning to leave town with," Dixie mused. "Maybe Dwayne …"

The three of us stilled and stood there in silence for several moments.

Dixie looked at me. "Sugar, you were just out there. What do you think?"

"Wait. You went there?" Max sputtered. "When?"

"A couple of days ago. I was trying to return this crazy box." I filled him in on the background of the family artifact and the reaction I'd gotten when I'd tried to give it to Dwayne.

He shook his head. "Did you know he might be dangerous?"

"No. And we still don't know if he is," I defended my view.

"Sugar is convinced that Dwayne isn't dangerous. Only hurt."

"That would be you." Max gave me a look.

"Though he did say something that now, with this new development, sounds more threatening than I thought it was at the time." I swallowed, thinking about the encounter.

"What did he say?"

"Something to the effect of I should tell Mame not to be digging up the past. Some things are better off left buried."

I looked at the two of them. "I guess I'd better share that with Sheriff Terry, huh?"

"Yes." Max's voice was low, and a muscle twitched in his cheek. "And when will that security camera you've ordered be here?"

Dixie and I looked at each other. "We're working on it," I answered.

"Also," I stopped as a thought hit me, "Mame told me that Dwayne blamed Marla when DeeDee disappeared because she'd said she was with Marla when she was actually meeting this guy."

Mame, maybe you were right and Dwayne is truly scary, after all.

Max bid us goodbye and, with Dixie's directions, left to join Sheriff Terry at the Darling Farm.

It would only be a matter of time before the news traveled like wildfire and made its way around the square. And through the rest of the town.

It was impossible to concentrate on the layout of the cookbook now. All I could think about was the body in Dwayne Darling's well. I found myself standing, staring off into space, my mind racing.

Good grief. This changed everything. Or maybe answered everything.

I wondered whether Mame knew. On the job at the school, she'd surely heard.

And what did this mean for Zac?

"You're going to wear a hole in that card if you keep rubbing your thumb over it," Dixie said, breaking into my thoughts.

I looked down to find I'd been tracing the same spot on

Mrs. Brennan's Irish Soda Bread over and over. "Sorry. I can't stop thinking about that body in the well."

"If it is Delores …" Dixie left the thought hanging, her eyes meeting mine across the table.

The bell above the front door dinged, and I turned to see Tina hurrying in, her stiletto heels clicking rapidly across our tile floor. The fall outfit of the day was a tan pencil skirt, a crimson blazer, and a scarf with a leaf motif.

"Ladies, you will not believe the latest," she announced, slightly out of breath.

"Let me guess," Dixie said. "News about a dead body at Dwayne Darling's farm?"

Tina's perfect eyebrows rose. "You already heard?"

"Uh-huh." Dixie pushed aside a stack of recipe cards to make room for Tina's oversized designer purse.

"But all we know is that they found a body in an abandoned well on the property," I clarified, giving Dixie a "Let the woman talk" look. Maybe Tina had more details than we had.

Tina leaned forward, lowering her voice even though no one else was there. "I've been told that Sheriff Griffin just brought Dwayne in for questioning."

I felt my stomach tighten. "They've identified the body already?"

"Not officially." Tina drummed her glittery, manicured fingers on the counter. "You know they have to go through all that forensic stuff."

I wasn't sure Tina knew what "all that forensic stuff" entailed. As an avid mystery reader, I felt like I had at least some understanding of what they had to go through. At least I knew it wasn't like on TV. It was going to take some time. Days, maybe weeks.

"Do they think it's Dwayne's wife, then?" Dixie asked.

"Here's the deal. Katie from the diner was delivering lunch to the station when they brought him in, and she said Deputy Butters told her they'd found a handbag with the body."

"A handbag?" My mind swirled with too many thoughts. "With ID?"

"Yep," Tina continued. "I wonder if the money she took is in there. You know she took money out of their accounts for months leading up to when she left—"

She stopped in the middle of her story.

"Only maybe she didn't leave," I finished for her. "Could it really be Delores after all this time?"

Tina nodded emphatically. "That's what everyone is guessing. You remember what I said about Dwayne being difficult over the Rural Water lines crossing his land a while back. Maybe he had something to hide."

"Maybe." I stood up, needing to move as my mind worked through the possibilities. "But why now? After ten years, why would the body suddenly be found now?"

"Right." Dixie speared fingers through her red curls. "Who called in the tip?"

I paced the length of the shop, my own theories bumping into each other. "So that means someone else knew or figured out that the body was there." I stopped by the window and looked out at the town square. The autumn sun was casting long shadows across the courthouse lawn, where a few people were gathered in groups. No doubt, the buzz had shifted from reality show filming to this shocking discovery.

Had Marla figured it out and that's what led to her death? But someone had called the tip in today. Did that mean someone else followed the same trail Marla had?

"You don't really think Dwayne is innocent, do you,

Sugar?" Tina asked, sounding a little disappointed that I might spoil a perfectly good scoop.

"I don't think anything yet." I turned to face Tina and Dixie. "But if that is Delores in the well … and she's been there for ten years … someone in St. Ignatius has been keeping a secret for a very long time." A shiver skittered up my spine.

"Geez Louise." Tina hefted her purse from the counter. "First Marla Mercer's murder, then the break-ins, and now this. That Hollywood film crew will be thinking they've wandered into the Twilight Zone."

She straightened her blazer, grabbed her bag off the counter, and clicked her way out the door.

"I'd think there's something more important about all of this than what the film crew thinks." Dixie shook her head as if to clear it.

"And I think somehow, with it being Delores and then Marla, the two must be related. But what does one murder have to do with the other? What are we missing?"

Zac had said he didn't have anything to do with Marla's death. And he had said he'd heard her arguing with a man. Did this confirm it was Dwayne Darling?

We tried hard but didn't accomplish much work the rest of the afternoon. And finally, Dixie and I made the decision to call it a day.

I stopped to pick up a few groceries on the way home. The discovery at the Darling Farm was the topic of conversion in every aisle. You could not get away from it.

When I finally pulled into my driveway, I didn't see any movement from next door. Mrs. Pickett should have been happy, as it seemed like Mame was in the clear. The sheriff had moved on and had two solid suspects as far as he was concerned. Neither of which I was, beyond any doubt, completely convinced about.

Letting myself in, I dropped my bags, fed Ernest, and changed his water. Then I collapsed on the couch.

Ermest appeared from the kitchen to check on me, licking his chops. He was clearly concerned about his roommate, but first things first, right?

"Meow?" he asked.

"I'm okay," I reassured him. Though emotionally, I was a wreck.

"You see, on the one hand, if Dwayne Darling killed his wife and then killed Marla, that will clear Zac."

"Meow," Ernest agreed with my reasonable conclusion.

"He'll still have the break-ins to face up to, but that will be much less serious. But why would Dwayne kill Marla now? Ten years later?"

I looked at the cat, mulling the questions.

Maybe Marla had found something? Mame had said she'd been going through things at the house. Maybe we needed to take another look around.

Was there something significant that we'd missed? Something that would implicate Dwayne? Proof he killed his wife?

Was that what the argument Zac had overheard had been about? If so, what had happened to the evidence?

"Meow," Ernest commented.

"I know. So many questions, right?"

Ernest got up from his spot and padded to the hallway. His expression said, "Time for a treat."

I lifted myself from the sofa. "And the anonymous caller. There's a loose end for you. Who made that phone call? And again, why now?"

The trill of the doorbell startled us both.

Please, please, not Mrs. Pickett.

I crept toward the door on tiptoe, trying to see who it was.

Peering out the side pane of the door, I huffed a sigh of relief. It was not Mrs. Pickett. It was Sheriff Terry. Opening the door, I waved him in.

"Got a minute?" he asked. "I stopped by the shop, but it looked like you and Dixie had locked up and gone home."

"We did." I stepped back so he could enter. "It was hard to concentrate with … well, everything."

"Yeah, that craziness with the film crew in town is something else. And then the discovery this morning …" His uniform was rumpled and smudged with grass stains.

As I closed the door behind him, I spotted the Jameson County Sheriff's Department car in my driveway. Great. Mrs. Pickett was going to have a heyday with that. "I was about to make myself a coffee. Would you like one?"

"If it's not any trouble, coffee would be great." He followed me into the kitchen and pulled out a chair to sit down at the table.

I made two cups of coffee and sat down across from him. "I have so many questions."

"I probably have the same ones you do, so don't expect any brilliant answers from me." He scrubbed his hands down his face and reached for the coffee cup.

"First off, is it Delores?" I leaned forward.

"We're pretty sure it is." Sheriff Terry leaned back and narrowed his eyes. "The handbag was in rough shape, but the driver's license survived."

"Plastic lasts forever." Taking a sip of coffee, I pictured the rectangle of plastic.

"Yeah. Almost." His head bobbed.

I waited for a couple of beats.

Here comes my big question. I trust Sheriff Terry's instincts and hope he'll give me a straight answer.

"Do you think Dwayne killed her?"

Sheriff Terry paused.

"He says not. And at this point, I don't have enough evidence to hold him. So he's out on the street, and I'm not happy about that."

"And what about Marla?"

I noted his slight look away and the neutral expression that dropped into place before he answered. "He admits he's been in contact with her but claims she reached out to him."

He was still law enforcement and wasn't going to spill everything, but his reaction was enough to tell me that they were working on something.

I glanced toward the window, where the afternoon light was spilling in and splintering as it hit the sun catcher in the window. My thoughts were as scattered as the light beams.

It still doesn't make sense.

"Why did you stop by?" I was sure it wasn't to make sure I knew about the discovery at the Darling Farm. Max had taken care of that. And Tina. Plus all those people at the grocery store.

"It's Mame Reinhart." He pushed back his chair and set his cup down. "She's really in a state, and I could use your help. The news about the body and the idea that it could be Delores hit her hard. And, of course, she heard it via the town grapevine."

"Not the ideal way to hear that kind of news." I stared across the room.

"It sure as hell isn't," he agreed. "The thing is, I think she needs checking on and she likes you. Would you check on her?"

"I'd be happy to." My phone buzzed, interrupting us. I picked it up and looked at the display. "And guess who this is?"

I held the phone so he could see it.

"Thank you," he whispered, getting up and taking his cup to the sink. "I'll let myself out."

Pushing the button to answer the call, I poured myself another coffee and sat back down at the table. "Mame, how are you doing?"

19

After talking with Mame for a while, I knew that an in-person visit was desperately needed. Sheriff Terry's assessment that she was "in a state" had undersold it. I called Dixie, and after filling her in, we decided to go together. Dixie agreed to pick me up, and I said I'd be ready.

She was in my driveway in thirty minutes.

Telling Ernest I'd be back soon, I kissed the top of his furry head. He was not pleased about the change in routine. Or the kiss, for that matter.

Stopping to lock my front door, I could see Mrs. Pickett on her front porch and waved. She glared and turned away. I didn't know what I'd done now, but I had bigger fish to fry.

"I'm glad you thought this was a good idea too," I said as I climbed into Dixie's truck. Or tried to climb in, as there was a foil-wrapped package on the passenger seat. "What's this?"

"I figured, with what you described from your phone call with Mame, she probably isn't eating." Dixie picked up the package so I could sit. "I thought we could take her something that might tempt her."

"As good as that smells, it may not make it there." I grinned, taking the warm bundle from Dixie and holding it to my nose. "You're probably right about Mame not eating. And you just whipped this up?"

"It's my Double-Glazed Lemon Loaf, and I usually make a few of them at a time and freeze them. I made a batch and had them cooling. I got the recipe from my cousin, Jana, who lives in Missouri. I'll write down the recipe for you if you want." She didn't go on, but her raised brow said, "It's so simple, even you could make it."

Or that's how I interpreted the look, anyway.

And she wasn't wrong about my culinary skills.

"It was really thoughtful of you to think about bringing something for her. I'm sure Mame will appreciate it."

It was a short trip to Marla's house, as I still thought of the place. And as Dixie pulled into the long drive, I wished she could see the interior of the main house. I wasn't sure, with the new discovery, whether the investigation into Delores's death would mean they'd go through things at Marla's house or not.

We parked in front of the carriage house and got out. I carried the warm bundle, and Dixie grabbed a small bag of paper plates and napkins she'd brought along.

"It's pretty back here." Dixie looked around as we approached the door. "What I wouldn't give to have this backyard."

"It is beautiful," I agreed.

Balancing the bread and my purse, I knocked. No answer. I exchanged glances with Dixie.

"Mame?" I called out. "It's Sugar and Dixie."

I knocked again, harder this time. After what seemed like forever, I heard shuffling footsteps. The door swung open to reveal Mame looking exhausted. Her eyes were red-rimmed, her hair was going every which way, and she still had on her work clothes.

I didn't wait for an invitation. "Look what Dixie made for you." I held up the loaf, sliding past her into the house.

"I figured you might be hungry and could use a treat," Dixie added, following me in.

I headed straight to the kitchen and stopped short at the sight of Mame's table. It was covered with journals—Marla's journals, I realized. There were stacks, some with sticky notes poking out from the pages.

Mame closed the door and hurried to join us. "I can move those."

"No need," I said, setting the lemon loaf on the counter. "Have you found anything in the journals?"

Mame sank into a chair at the table, her shoulders slumped in defeat. Her hands—so swift and steady when she was crocheting—trembled as she touched one of the books.

"Nothing that will help." She sighed. "I remembered conversations Marla and I had back when DeeDee left." She rubbed her forehead. "Disappeared," she corrected herself.

"You said before that Delores had sort of distanced herself. And you and Marla thought she was busy with her real estate work, right?" I sat down in the chair next to Mame.

"Exactly, but then I got to thinking maybe Marla knew more and it was only me who thought that about DeeDee. I decided to read through Marla's journals and see if I could find anything from around the time DeeDee disappeared."

"And did you have any luck?" Dixie asked, joining us at the table.

"Yes and no." Mame leaned her elbows on the table and propped her chin on her hands. "Her daily entries are short.

Only a few lines each day. And ten years ago, around the time, you know, when DeeDee went missing, there isn't much, but there are a couple of notes that make me feel like Marla knew DeeDee was up to something."

"And this entry." She picked up one of the books that had a yellow sticky note and turned it so we could see.

"She's gone," it said.

"Do you have the most recent journal?" I asked.

"No." Mame dropped her head into her hands. "It wasn't with the others. I can't believe DeeDee is dead. Was dead this whole time. And then Marla …" Her voice cracked.

I caught Dixie's look across the table, seeing my own concern mirrored on her face.

"Let's take a little break and have something to eat. Then we'll help you look some more." Dixie rose from the table. Then, as at home, as if it were her own kitchen, she found a serving knife.

I got out the paper plates and napkins. Dixie cut slices of the fragrant, sweet bread. And in a short time, we had Mame nibbling on the treat and talking about her job at the school.

As we talked and ate, Mame seemed to regroup and find her resolve again.

It was never good to be alone in grief, and it didn't matter whether it was a family member or a friend you were grieving; sometimes, you simply needed someone to be with you.

The lemon loaf was amazing, and we made quick work of the cleanup thanks to Dixie's paper plates. We moved to the living room, and Mame showed Dixie some of her crocheting.

I noticed the photo of Marla, Delores, and Mame on the small bench by the door. "That's you three together, isn't it?"

Mame smiled. "I brought it over from Marla's house."

"It's a great photo." I picked it up and carried it over to show Dixie.

The three friends smiling at the camera, their arms around each other's shoulders. Marla, the neat brunette. Delores, the vivacious, curly-haired blonde. And Mame, her round face and short hair not a lot different from today.

I handed the picture to Dixie. "How long ago was this?" she asked.

"Oh, probably twenty years ago." Mame shook her head. "Feels like forever."

Dixie handed the picture back to me, and I placed it back on the bench beside the brown satchel handbag it had been leaning against.

"I wish we'd taken more photos." Mame's eyes filled. "They were good friends. Now I'm the only one left." Tears spilled down her cheeks, and she grabbed the bag from beside her chair, pulled out a tissue, and mopped her face. "Sorry."

"Don't be sorry, hon." Dixie got up and went over to hug her. "It's hard."

"Is that your purse?" I asked.

Dixie gave me a hard look. A "What is the matter with you?" look.

"What?" Mame sniffed.

"Is that your purse?" I indicated the bag on her lap.

"Yes." Her voice was flat. "Why?"

"Then whose purse is that?" I pointed at the one on the bench by the door.

"That's Marla's." Now she was frowning at me along with Dixie. "Remember, I told you the sheriff gave it to me but I didn't feel right going through someone else's …

I could tell when it dawned on her.

"The journal." I picked up the bag. "Did you look in Marla's purse for the last journal?"

"No, I didn't."

I brought the purse to her.

"I still can't." She handed it back to me. "You look."

I sat down and opened the bag, pulling out sunglasses, a wallet, and breath mints. A packet of tissues, a tube of lipstick, and … I knew as soon as I touched it. Marla's journal. It matched the others.

Smiling at Mame and Dixie, I asked, "Shall we?"

They nodded, and we returned to our places at the table. I opened the journal to the last entry. The day before Marla was killed.

I looked up and read, "Tomorrow, I meet with him."

"No name?" Dixie asked.

I shook my head.

Dixie reached across the table and took Mame's hand. "What about the entries leading up to that day?"

I flipped back slowly through the previous pages, careful to make sure I reviewed each one carefully. "This one says, 'Now I know.'"

"Know what?" Mame speared her fingers through her hair, making it stand up even more. "Know what?"

I felt the same way. It was so frustrating. But how could Marla have known we'd be looking to her journal for answers? She must not have realized how much danger she was in.

Going back further to the weeks before Marla's death, I found only two more entries that seemed as if they might be related to what she'd discovered. One said, "It was there all along." And an earlier one noted, "I will figure this out."

The rest of the days were filled with what she'd done that

day and notes about her garden or, occasionally, a book she was enjoying. Marla's life emerged in the daily chronicling.

I laid the book on the table. "She didn't talk to you about anything she was looking into or mention trying to figure something out?"

"I can't remember anything like that." Mame shook her head. "Nothing."

The three of us sat in silence for several minutes.

"If you haven't already told the sheriff about these"—I swept my hand toward the journals—"you probably should."

"I will." She stood and began gathering them into a pile.

Dixie rose and began clearing the table. "I'll leave you the rest of this." She rewrapped the remaining bread.

In a short time, we had cleaned up and were ready to take our leave.

"Thank you." Mame hugged me and then Dixie. "For the food and for helping me feel less alone."

"You lock up after us, and if you need anything, you call." I gave her an extra squeeze.

On the trip back to my house, Dixie and I talked through our time at Mame's and what a shame it was that Marla's journals had not been more help. It was so disappointing.

Waving goodbye to Dixie, I climbed my porch steps to find a plastic skeleton lounging on my porch swing. Not exactly the fall décor I'd had in mind.

I looked for a note, sure that Mrs. Pickett was somehow involved, but found nothing.

"I'll deal with you later," I told him and let myself in.

Ernest was again confused by the change in routine and thought we should repeat the coming home ritual of head pets, fresh water, food, and treats.

"I'm not falling for it," I told him.

I'd heard people use the term "done in," and that was how I felt. I was spent physically, mentally, and emotionally. My head hurt, and though I hadn't done my morning run in days —or even an evening walk, for that matter—my energy was zapped.

Dropping my bag by the door, I dragged myself upstairs and changed into my "Cat Nap" pajama pants and a T-shirt. No matter how dire the circumstances, this would not have been a look that my mother would approve of. Not under any circumstances.

I mean, what if someone comes to your door, Sugar?

I didn't care. If someone did, it would probably be Mrs. Pickett. And tonight, I was all about comfort. Dixie had given me the pajama pants for Christmas, and I loved them.

I padded downstairs and flipped on the television. My usual fare was either British baking or detective shows, but I wasn't sure whether my favorites had any new episodes. Lately, I'd been watching a genealogy show that researched people's ancestry. It was fascinating, and I often picked up tips I could use in my own research. It looked as if a new install-ment was available, so I queued it up and headed to the kitchen for some snacks.

Ernest followed me, complaining.

I caved. If I was going to have treats, it was only fair that he should too.

Finally, I snuggled into the couch pillows. Snacks, check. Fuzzy blanket, check. Satisfied cat, check.

Settling in, I started the show, hoping it would be a distraction. If it pulled me in and took me away for a little while, it would have served its purpose.

No thinking about a kid in trouble, a missing woman, or murder. Not for a couple of hours, anyway.

The show was interesting, but it was so difficult to concentrate, and though I thought I'd been paying attention, I must have drifted off.

I woke up to a different show. One about antiques. Since this show was on location in the Midwest, the host was talking to a historian about how families brought furniture and heirlooms from Europe and eventually transported them to their new homes on the prairie.

And the techniques they used to keep their valuables safe on the trip west.

That's when it hit me.

The link between Delores and Marla. I didn't know what Marla had found, but I thought I knew where she'd found it.

And, boy, did I hope I was right.

20

With all of my being, I hoped I was right.

If I was, we could finally answer what had happened to Delores. And know what Marla had discovered that got her killed.

Pulling into the deserted parking lot at the shop, I got out and hit the button to lock my car. I made sure I had my cell phone. If I was right, this couldn't wait until morning.

I'd give Sheriff Terry a call. Immediately.

I grabbed my bag and headed for the back door. I unlocked it and entered. Flipping the light on in my office, I headed to the storeroom. The storeroom where, a few days ago, Dixie, Terry, and Disco had been telling knock-knock jokes. I shook my head at the craziness of the past few days. The past several weeks.

The wooden box was sitting right where I'd shoved it.

Picking it up, I carried it into the kitchen, where the light was better, and put it on the island. Taking a tea towel and brushing off the top with its lovely folk art carving, I wondered about the history. Had the girl whose face adorned the box been an ancestor of Delores? Maybe a beloved sweet-heart, a wife-to-be, a sister, a friend.

I turned it around on the granite countertop and looked at it closely, walking my fingers around the edges.

"Come on," I whispered. "Give up your secrets."

My fingers found the catch—a small indentation almost invisible under the lip. I pressed it, but it was rusty and wouldn't budge. I picked up Dixie's fancy cake tester from the utensil holder and pushed it against the spot, and it gave. I heard the release and lifted out the false bottom.

I couldn't believe what I was looking at.

Money. Bundles of money. Lots of bundles. I lifted the first layer, and there was more. A small card with a note on the back of it was stuck to one side. Picking it up and peering at the faded ink, I sucked in a breath.

"Meet me at the usual spot," it said.

I recognized the handwriting and the signature.

Suddenly, I heard a footfall behind me and I jumped.

"Well, look at how clever you are, Sugar." Lewis Brimley stepped out of the shadows and into the kitchen.

Where did he come from?

My heart slammed against my ribs. "Lewis, you scared me." I steadied myself against the counter, my hands trembling. "What are you doing here?"

"Let's see what you've got there." He stepped forward toward me, and I caught a glint of something in his hand. "Good thing I decided to follow you."

That's when I heard the chilling racking of a shotgun from the doorway Lewis had just come through.

"And a good thing I did too," said a voice from the shadows. "You stay back."

Dwayne Darling stepped forward into the room, holding a

shotgun, the stock against his shoulder and the barrel pointed at Lewis.

"You don't want to do that, Dwayne," I said quietly, hoping to diffuse a situation that I currently couldn't see any way out of.

"Oh, I most sincerely do, Sugar," Dwayne answered, his voice deep and as steady as his aim. He stepped further into the room, advancing toward Lewis.

"You don't understand." Lewis's face paled, and he fidgeted with what I could now see was a knife in his hand.

"I understand plenty," Dwayne countered.

I looked around for a weapon of my own, but Dixie had cleaned up and put everything away.

Or a way out would be good.

If I could get to my cell phone, which was in my purse in the office, I could call 9-1-1. I gauged the distance to the door, but it was blocked by Dwayne.

"It was an accident." Lewis's gaze darted between us, calculating. "She fell—"

"Don't," Dwayne bit out. "Don't you dare." His finger tightened on the trigger.

Lewis raised the knife and lunged toward me, grabbing for the note, his face contorted in desperation. "Give me that."

"No!" I jammed the note in the pocket of my pajama pants. "So that's what you've been looking for?" All the going through papers, asking what Marla had given me, bugging Mame. It had all been about finding that note.

"I didn't know what I was looking for. She taunted me," he bit out. "Said she had 'proof' but wouldn't tell me what proof. Stupid meddler, like you—" The knife glittered in his hand as he raised it again.

The blade sliced down, and I ducked, banging my head hard on the sharp edge of the island.

He grabbed again, his hand connecting with the box this time. I raised up and shoved against his knees as hard as I could. The force sent the box flying and money skittering across the floor.

With an umph, Lewis fell against the tall kitchen shelves, and cookbooks rained down on us both.

Dwayne surged forward, tackling Lewis and forcing him to the floor.

The room seemed to tilt and narrow. My ears were ringing and my head was throbbing, but I thought I heard sirens. My legs gave out, and I sank to the floor.

Dwayne looked at me. "You okay?"

I nodded. "Did you call the police?"

"Nope," he answered. "Did you?"

I started to shake my head, but it hurt too much. I touched it, and it felt sticky.

"You might want to grab a towel." He pointed. "That's a lot of blood."

I grabbed the closest kitchen towel and applied pressure on what I was sure was a very small puncture wound. Then, finally giving up, I tied it so it would stay.

I could hear the shouts as they came through the back door.

Sheriff Terry, along with two deputies, burst into the room.

And stopped cold.

I was sure it was a sight. Dwayne with his shotgun by his side, holding Lewis Brimley pinned to the floor.

Me in my cat pajama pants, a kitchen towel dotted with cows and daisies wrapped around my head like a turban.

And bucketloads of money scattered the length of the room.

DIXIE HADN'T BEEN FAR BEHIND SHERIFF TERRY AND THE deputies. She sat down beside me on the floor and removed the kitchen towel to take a look at my head.

"Can you get up?" She stood and reached out.

"I think so." I took her hand and got to my feet.

"Let's go back to the office and get the first aid kit." She linked her arm with mine. "And then you can fill me in on what brought you here in the middle of the night, where all that money came from, and who's who in the murder mystery it appears you have solved."

"Good idea." I nodded and then stopped. "Ouch."

Sheriff Terry joined us, still arguing that I needed a trip to the ER. I filled him and Dixie in on how I'd come up with the idea that maybe the thing we'd been missing was the importance of the antique box. The box that had been at the historical society, at Lewis's office, and at Marla's house and that Dwayne had been so adamant he didn't want.

I gave the sheriff the note that'd been in the box with the money. Lewis, it seemed, was still claiming it was all an accident. That when he'd gone to meet Delores at the well, she had fallen.

Yeah, no. I don't think so.

His face and the flash of that knife were still fresh in my mind.

There was still a lot of work to be done to piece everything together, but I was certain, based on how the events had unfolded tonight, he was guilty of both murders.

"I have a question." I looked from Dixie to Sheriff Terry and back. "How did you know to come?"

Dixie smiled and held up her phone. "The security cameras came, and Hirsh went ahead and put them up this afternoon while we were at Mame's. He stopped by and showed me how to connect it to my phone. When you went in the back door, it notified me."

"And she notified me." The sheriff grinned.

Thank goodness for Hirsh and tech, or things might have turned out differently.

Dixie patched me up with the gauze and tape from the first aid kit. Sheriff Terry went to follow up on securing the kitchen so it could be processed. Dwayne had removed the shells from his shotgun and handed it over to one of the deputies. Lewis had been cuffed, read his rights, and put in one of the cars out back.

There was still a lot to be sorted out.

"Did you convince her to visit the ER?" he asked Dixie as he passed by.

"No luck," she replied. "She's very hardheaded this one."

"No kidding." He looked me over. "Would you like to go home? We can get your statement later."

"I would love to go home." I stood, reached for my bag, and fished out my keys.

"No, you don't." The sheriff plucked the keys from my hand and tossed them to Dixie.

I didn't argue.

Right now, nothing sounded better than my bossy feline, my own bed, and sleep.

"Come on, Sugar Ray." Dixie looped her arm through mine. "Let's get you home."

The morning of the St. Ignatius Fall Festival, Dixie and I were in the shop early. Like zero dark thirty early. Mame had been helping with the cookie baking and was now assisting with the boxing. We had five dozen cookies to get to the YAP kids for the skate park fundraiser. Their booth was across the way on the courthouse lawn. We made short work of handing off the cookies to Hirsh and Zac, who were currently staffing the booth.

Zac wasn't in the clear, but none of the business owners who'd had money stolen wanted to press charges. Zac was working for Hirsh part time at his construction company and had agreed to pay everything back.

A typical fall chill was hanging in the air, and after our cookie delivery, we staked out prime curbside viewing spots right in front of our shop to watch the parade. We were set with lawn chairs, blankets, and a thermos of hot apple cider. Mame had crocheted us orange hats to keep our ears warm, and we immediately put them on. I was careful as I snugged mine down on my head, avoiding the lump on my temple, which, though better, was still a bit tender.

I love, love, love parades.

Spaces along the curb on each side of us began to fill up, and most onlookers were also bundled up against the cold. Many, like us, had lawn chairs and blankets. I inhaled, savoring the scents of freshly popped kettle corn, hot baked cinnamon rolls, and crispy fried apple pies as booths began to open. Though it seemed too early in the day for me, a little guy in a pumpkin hoodie who belonged to the family group next to us was chomping on a corn dog.

I could see them setting up for the chili cook-off on the opposite side of the courthouse green space. It was being judged by Mayor Kirby, Toy George, and—big surprise— celebrity chef Dino Diner, who'd given the Red Hen Diner nothing but compliments during his filming there.

I'd had a conversation with Dino the day before, and he'd apologized for the incident that may or may not have gotten me fired. It turned out that the morning he'd come to the shop, he'd been there to tell me he was sorry. Before he was interrupted by Sheriff Terry. It also turned out he was responsible for the hundred-dollar bill that had shown up in the donation jar.

Wow. I did not see that one coming.

I was sitting wrapped in my warm, cozy blanket, taking in my surroundings. The sun had finally broken through the clouds, the dome of the courthouse reflecting the light. The crowd buzzed with excitement as it came time for the parade. We could hear it before it got to us, the marching band in front, the bass drums setting the tempo, then the rest of the percussion, the brass, and the woodwinds joining in. Their spiffy new uniforms provided by the band boosters looked sharp.

Next up was a group of cute little dancers dressed as harvest fairies, all gold and glittery with antennae on their heads topped with autumn leaves. Because of the cold, most of them had coats on over their fairy outfits, but they were still adorable, and you could hear the collective "awww" of the people along the route as they passed by.

One of the city fire engines had been conscripted to participate and periodically ran its siren to the delight of the crowd. There were a number of floats representing sports teams, businesses, and community groups, but my favorite was the float for The Good Life, which held Greer and some of the other residents. Attired in skeleton onesies, they did a lively twist and shout routine to "Monster Mash," their silver heads bopping.

The winner of the biggest pumpkin contest followed on a flatbed behind the floats. It certainly was the biggest pumpkin I'd ever seen. Probably bigger than that giant popcorn ball Greer and her gang had gone to see.

Finishing up the parade were the St. Ignatius Harvest King and Queen, who had been crowned at a ceremony last night. Frank Donaldson was ninety-seven, and Bessie Allen was ninety-nine. They were sitting proudly in the back of a red convertible, waving at all of the people lining the square, their gold crowns slightly askew and royal robes wrapped around them. We waved back.

After that, the crowd began to break up, heading toward the booths for a favorite snack or activity. Max stopped by to chat for a few minutes before he had to get to the chili cook-off to take photos of the winners. Shouldering his camera bag to leave, he leaned in with a cautious kiss on the cheek, skillfully avoiding my injured spot, and a promise to check in again later.

Most of the people had moved on, but Mame, Dixie, and I continued to sit in our lawn chairs, chatting and sipping our cider, not in a big rush to get anywhere.

A sense of contentment settled over me like a warm hug. My adopted hometown was back to normal. Well, almost back to normal, anyway.

Lewis Brimley had been charged and was awaiting trial. Sheriff Terry had told us that when they'd dug into his past, they'd found that his first wife had died under suspicious circumstances.

It seemed, from what the sheriff had pieced together, Lewis had targeted Delores. But at the last minute, she had changed her mind about leaving Dwayne and met Lewis at the well to tell him. I wasn't sure we'd ever know all the details for certain. But for Dwayne Darling's sake, I hoped that part of the story was true.

"Have you decided anything more about services?" Dixie asked Mame.

"We're planning a joint memorial service in two weeks for both Marla and DeeDee," she answered. "Dwayne agreed."

"I may need your help," she added, straightening her hat.

"Of course," Dixie responded. "We'd be happy to help."

"I'm so glad we got to know your friends through you, Mame." I smiled at Mame, tucking the blanket around my knees.

"And the one good thing to come out of this is I got to know you two as friends." Mame leaned back in her chair.

"And we got to know you," Dixie chimed in.

"How about a toast to Marla and DeeDee?" I suggested. "The two who brought us together."

Dixie topped off our cups of spiced apple cider, and we raised them in salute. "To Marla and DeeDee." Mame's voice cracked a little as she said their names.

"And one more toast," I said, smiling at the other two. "To friends."

Leaning in, we straightened our orange hats, touched our cups of cider together with a pretend clink, and toasted one more time. "To friends!"

PART I

RECIPES FROM THE BOOK

GREER GOODER'S EASY HOMEMADE BREAD

Ingredients

1 pkg (¼ oz) active dry yeast
2¼ c warm water
3 tbsp sugar (plus ½ tsp)
1 tbsp salt
2 tbsp oil (canola works well)
6¼ to 6¾ c bread flour

Instructions

1. Preheat the oven to 375°F. Grease two 9" x 5" loaf pans.
2. Dissolve the yeast and the ½ tsp of sugar in the warm water.
3. Let stand until bubbles form on the surface.
4. Whisk together 3 c of flour plus the salt and remaining 3 tbsp of sugar.

5. Stir the oil into the yeast mixture.
6. Pour the yeast mixture into the flour mixture and beat until smooth.
7. Stir in more of the remaining flour, ½ c at a time, until you have a soft dough.
8. Turn the dough onto a floured surface and knead until smooth.
9. Place in a greased glass bowl, turning once to coat the top.
10. Cover and let rise in a warm place until doubled. Approximately 1½ to 2 hrs.
11. Punch down, turn onto a lightly floured surface, divide in half, and place in loaf pans.
12. Place in loaf pans and let rise until doubled. Again, approximately 1½ to 2 hrs.
13. Bake until golden brown and the bread sounds hollow when tapped.
14. Remove from pans and cool on a wire rack.

Notes

Greer says to make sure you check the date on your yeast. You can proof it by mixing it with warm water and a pinch of sugar to see whether it bubbles. If it does, it's still alive and active.

The times for letting your bread rise are approximate, as different environments can affect the timing. For best results, make sure your dough is covered and placed in a warm (80–85°), draft-free area, and leave it alone.

Punching down the dough means pressing your fist quickly but gently into the center of the dough, forming it into a ball, and then kneading it two to three times.

DIXIE SPICER'S BLONDE BROWNIES

Ingredients

1 c butter, melted
1¼ c brown sugar
2 eggs
2 tsp vanilla
2 tsp baking powder
1 tsp baking soda
2 c flour
½ c chocolate chips

Instructions

1. Preheat the oven to 350°F. Line a 9" x 13" pan or spray with nonstick spray. Set aside.
2. Combine the butter and brown sugar in a bowl.
3. Add the eggs and vanilla and mix well.
4. Combine the dry ingredients.
5. Add to the previous mixture.

6. Stir in the chocolate chips.
7. Pour the batter into the 9" x 13" pan.
8. Bake for 20–25 mins or until lightly brown.
9. Remove from the oven and cool completely.
10. Slice and serve.

Notes

You can add additional ingredients like nuts, butterscotch chips, toffee, or caramel bits for a slightly different taste. Dixie suggests trying the basic recipe first and then experimenting with various other flavors.

Sugar loves the basic chocolate chip version, as does Sheriff Terry, though he says they are best warm right out of the oven and served with a scoop of ice cream.

SHAKLEE FAMILY DEPRESSION CORN BREAD

Ingredients

1¼ c flour
1¼ c cornmeal
2 large eggs
⅓ c sugar (or honey)
1 tbsp baking powder
1 tsp salt
1 c milk
⅓ c oil

Instructions

1. Preheat the oven to 400°F and grease a 10" cast-iron skillet with 2 tbsp of oil.
2. Combine the flour, cornmeal, sugar, baking powder, and salt. Mix well.
3. Combine the eggs, milk, and oil. Mix well.

4. Add the wet ingredients to the dry ingredients and
   blend.
5. Pour into the cast-iron skillet and bake for 20–25
   mins or until golden brown.

Notes

A baking sheet can be used in place of a cast-iron skillet if you
prefer.

ST. IGNATIUS BAND BOOSTERS' CRUNCH & MUNCH

Ingredients

For the base:
½ c popcorn kernels (for 4 qt popped)
2 tbsp canola oil
2 tbsp unsalted butter
Large pinch of kosher salt
3 c nuts (any combination of peanuts, pecan halves, almonds, cashews, and walnuts)

For the ooey-gooey part:
½ c light Karo corn syrup
1 c well-packed light brown sugar
1½ sticks of unsalted butter, cut into chunks

Instructions

1. Preheat the oven to 250°F and spray a large rimmed baking sheet with nonstick spray.

2. Melt a half stick of unsalted butter and reserve for later.
3. Pop the corn using the canola oil, add the 2 tbsp of butter, toss, and salt.
4. Top with the nuts and set aside.
5. Melt the stick of butter in a saucepan, add brown sugar and corn syrup.
6. Bring to a boil, stirring constantly with a wooden spoon.
7. Reduce heat to medium and boil for 5 mins.
8. Quickly pour the hot mixture over the popcorn, stirring to distribute.
9. Add the reserved butter while stirring.
10. Turn out onto the baking sheet and bake for 1 hr, stirring every 15 mins.
11. Transfer to a cool baking sheet to dry and set.
12. Delicious served slightly warm but can be stored.

Notes

Parchment paper works as well if you'd prefer to use it instead of nonstick spray. Also, the band booster moms say the key to making the best Crunch & Munch is to work quickly. It's important to get the popcorn fully coated before the caramel sauce hardens.

Also, for best results, homemade popcorn gives you more flavor, but you can substitute microwave popcorn in a pinch. Most brands' regular bags yield 3½ to 4 c, so you'd need four to five bags.

JANA DOBSON'S DOUBLE GLAZED LEMON LOAF

Ingredients

For the loaf:
1 small box instant lemon pudding (3 oz)
1 c water
1 box lemon cake mix
4 large eggs
1 tsp lemon extract
⅓ c canola or vegetable oil

For the glaze:
¼ cup fresh lemon juice
Powdered sugar to desired consistency
Lemon zest

Instructions

1. Preheat the oven to 350°F. Grease with shortening,

then flour two 9" x 5" loaf pans or a 10-c Bundt pan. You can use spray if you prefer.

2. Combine the cake mix with the pudding.
3. Add 1 c water and ⅓ cup oil and mix slowly with your mixer.
4. Add the eggs one at a time.
5. Add the lemon extract.
6. Mix for 2 mins at medium speed.
7. Pour the cake batter into the prepared pan and bake for 45 mins or until a toothpick comes out clean or with a few moist crumbs.
8. Allow the cake to cool in the pan on a wire rack for 10–15 mins, then turn it out onto a cake plate or cooling rack to cool completely.

For the glaze: In a small bowl, mix the lemon juice and powdered sugar. Slowly drizzle the glaze over the top of the cake. The cake can still be slightly warm when you do this. Once the cake has cooled completely and the first glaze has dried, glaze again. After it has cooled and dried completely, store the cake in an airtight container at room temperature.

Notes

These loaves freeze well. Though if you're going to freeze them, Jana recommends freezing without the glaze. When you're ready to use the loaf, you can let it thaw at room temperature and then glaze.

ACKNOWLEDGMENTS

Some stories write their own themes and this story was one of those. As the story unfolded in my head and I worked to get it down in words, it became clear this was more than a cozy mystery with its quirky small-town characters and charming setting. It was also at its core a story about friendships.

So let me first say how deeply grateful I am for my long-time friends and critique partners, Tami, Cindy, Christine, and Anita. Your steadfast encouragement and fabulous feedback were invaluable.

A bucket load of gratitude to my best friend, my husband, Tim. And to my family for your love, understanding, and endless support. It takes a special family to discuss murder methods and plot twists at family gatherings.

Thank-you to my agent, Christine Witthohn, at Book Cents Literary Agency for her expert guidance, generous encouragement, and pit bull support. And who I also count as a friend.

I'm also grateful to Oliver Heber Books and especially to Tanya Ann Crosby for her leadership and inspiration. And to Sue-Ellen Welfonder for her wonderful editorial input. We are simpatico in so many ways and I love all the ways you made this a better book. And to Keri Maniquet for her editing/proofing expertise.

And finally, a heartful thank you to my readers. My book

friends - some of whom I've met in person and others who I've only met online but feel like I know anyway. Thank you for your notes and emails that let me know Sugar, Dixie, and the rest of the crew come alive for you. Thank you for your encouragement, your recipes, and your friendship!

Mary Lee Ashford is a lifelong bibliophile, an avid reader, and supporter of public libraries. In addition to writing the Sugar and Spice series for Oliver Heber Books, she also writes the Pampered Pets mystery series as half of the writing team of Sparkle Abbey. Prior to publishing Mary Lee won first place in the Daphne du Maurier contest and was a finalist in Murder in the Grove's mystery contest, as well as Killer Nashville's Claymore Dagger contest.

She is the founding president of Sisters in Crime – Iowa and a former board member of the Mystery Writers of America Midwest chapter, as well as a member of Novelists, Inc., and Sisters in Crime.

She loves encouraging writers and is a frequent lecturer and workshop presenter for writers' groups. Mary Lee has a long-time interest in creativity and teaches a university level course in Creative Management, as well as presenting workshops and blogging about creativity.

She currently resides in the Midwest with her husband, Tim, and Zoey, her feline coworker. When not writing her passions are reading, travel, and time with her family, especially her six grandchildren.

For more information, visit her website
at: www.MaryLeeAshford.com